absolutely worthy

D1377531

LaureL
shadrach
series
4

absolutely worthy

stephanie perry moore

MOODY PUBLISHERS
CHICAGO

Library of Congress Cataloging-in-Publication Data

Moore, Stephanie Perry.
    Absolutely worthy / Stephanie Perry Moore.
        p. cm. — (Laurel Shadrach series ; 4)
    Summary: In her freshman year of college, Laurel tries to stay true to her
Christian values while dealing with roommates, boyfriends, and pledging a sorority.
    ISBN 0-8024-4038-X
    [1. Chrisitian life—Fiction. 2. Colleges and universities—Fiction.]
I. Title. II. Series.

PZ7.M788125Ab 2003
[Fic]--dc21

                                                                    2003005725

3 5 7 9 10 8 6 4 2

Printed in the United States of America

For my nephews,
Kadarius Rochester Moore
&
Franklin Dennis Perry III

You two little men
mean so much to me.
As you grow, remember you
can achieve all your dreams.
Don't forget that with God all things are possible.
With the Lord on your side,
you can do anything.

contents

acknowledgments

I got some really bad news today. The little boy that I desperately wanted to adopt was given to another lady. I had wanted to be his mom for almost a year, but my husband felt it just wasn't the right time for our family. Depression, anger, resentment, and pain filled my soul. In the midst of my sorrow, I asked God why I didn't get the desire of my heart. Truly I felt the answer was that I was undeserving of such an awesome blessing. So if you've ever felt that God can't bless you because you're unworthy . . . I know how that feels.

But hold on, that's not the end of my story. Through counsel and prayer, I was reminded that God blesses me all the time despite myself. He sent His son to die for my sins. I could never be worthy of that gift. However, through His unconditional love, He saved me anyway. Such is the same with all that He provides. He is my Shepherd and He takes care of me, not because of what I do, but just because I'm His.

So to those of you unsure of who you are, sad, down, or simply just going through hard times, this book was written to give you hope. Yes, God wants us to be like Him. And we should strive for Christian perfection. But the truth is none of us will be perfect until we're in Heaven. Release all the negative feelings you have of yourself and believe that when God allows one door in your life to close, somewhere He'll open a window.

Believe in God, believe in yourself, and believe in your dreams. Things in life may not always work out the way you'd like, but when you turn it over to God, He works things out for the best. Take my situation—even though I won't be able to love on that little boy, Jermaine Woods from Connecticut finally has a family. And I'm getting excited to see where God is going to channel all the love that is in my heart. Like He didn't leave Jermaine, He won't leave you and me.

To all who give my writing wings to fly: my parents, Dr. Franklin and Shirley Perry, Sr.; my publishing company, Moody Publishers, especially Janis Backing; my reading pool—Kathleen Hanson, Sarah Hunter, Laurel Kasay, Carol Shadrach, and Marietta Shadrach; my assistants, Nakia Austin, Nicole Duncan, Courtney Manning, and Ashley Morgan; my Bible study group, the Coaches' Wives of the Georgia Tech Football Team; my daughters, Sydni and Sheldyn; my husband, Derrick Moore; and most importantly, my Lord, Jesus Christ—Your love makes me feel worthy. *Thanks to you all, I feel like an eagle soaring in the literary world making a difference for God.*

o n e

recapping
senior year

"What was that?" I screamed, startled out of a deep slumber by a loud buzzing noise.

"It's your alarm," a mouse-pitched voice complained.

I smacked the snooze button on my bedside clock and stared at the blurry numbers in the darkness. Surely it wasn't four o'clock! I blinked several times and the numbers grew clearer, but they didn't change. *What was I thinking?* I buried my head in the pillow and tried to shake off my drowsiness enough to figure out where I was.

When the mouse-pitched voice said, "Go back to sleep," I realized the speaker was Payton Skky, my college roommate. Payton and I had tried to stay up all night chatting about the common bonds we shared, like our faith in Jesus Christ and the exciting freshman year awaiting us. But somewhere in the course of our conversation, we'd both fallen asleep.

I rolled onto my back, and for the first time I noticed an

amazing array of glittery glow-in-the-dark stars on my dorm room ceiling. I took that as a sign that God was watching over me in my transition from adolescence to adulthood.

Lord, I know You're up there, I thought. *But I feel awfully insecure down here. I don't really know who I am anymore.*

The confident part of me replied, *What are you talking about, Laurel Shadrach? You're an awesome girl with style and class and charisma. You're beautiful, brilliant, bubbly, and bright.*

The not-so-confident part of me said, *That's not me. It sounds more like Jewels, the girl on the other side of that wall. Or the sorority girls at the frat party last night. There's nothing special about me.*

Nonsense, I argued with myself. *Think about where you've been. The experiences you went through during the past year have turned you into a dynamic person.*

That was a good point, I had to admit. I had gone through a lot in a short time. As a high school senior, I was the top gymnast in the entire state of Georgia. I was expected to compete on the U.S. gymnastics team in the Olympics. But then I sprained my ankle and cost my team the championship.

As a senior, I'd had the boy every girl in my school wanted—Branson Price, the captain and starting quarterback of the football team. I'd been sure we'd stay together all year and that our relationship would only deepen after graduation. But when I refused to go all the way with him, he dumped me and turned to someone else—my best friend, Brittany Cox.

I went out with Foster McDowell for a while. He was a great Christian guy, and he treated me like a princess. But I couldn't stop thinking about my ex. We finally broke up but remained good friends.

The image of Brittany making out with Branson under the school stairs continued to bother me. That girl had everything. Money. A great body. She was on the cheerleading squad. I'd often envied her. And yet, she told me she hooked up with Branson because *she* wanted what I had.

Our friendship ended for a while, but then tragedy struck her life. An ex-boyfriend she used to mess with contracted AIDS. Most of my other friends thought it was perfect justice for Brittany and Branson since they hurt me so badly. But God softened my heart toward both of them, and our friendships started to mend.

When Branson's AIDS tests came back negative, he pleaded for my forgiveness and begged me to be his girlfriend again. But I told him he had to stand on his own and so did I. We both made it into the University of Georgia, but I was determined to start a new life without him.

Brittany wasn't as fortunate as Branson. Her AIDS test was positive. She thought at first that was the end for her. But I helped her through that rough time, encouraging her to look to God for purpose and meaning in her life. She applied to the University of Florida and was accepted. I wondered if she was lying on her dorm room bed thinking about me.

I drifted off to sleep but was again rudely awakened by my alarm. Snooze time was over.

I needed to get to the gym and practice if I hoped to earn a spot on the Gym Dawgs gymnastics team.

I crawled out of bed and tiptoed to the small refrigerator in the corner of our room, my mouth watering for the chocolate milk I'd seen Payton put in the night before, along with sodas and snacks and—

"What?" I cried out when I saw the refrigerator was empty.

"What's wrong?" Payton screamed, sitting up in her bed.

"Sorry I woke you," I said. "But I wanted to have a quick breakfast before practice."

Payton fell back into her mattress with a moan.

"Where's all our stuff?" I asked before she could go back to sleep.

"I think Jewels took it all," Payton snarled as she punched her pillow.

"Why would you think that?"

"Because she saw me loading the fridge," Payton said. "And because it sounds like something she'd do."

I couldn't argue with that. I'd only known Jewels for a few days, but she reminded me a lot of my spoiled high school girlfriend, Brittany. Both girls were demanding, self-centered, sneaky, and beautiful. Jewels's dorm room was connected to ours by an adjoining bathroom, and I'd often heard her use some pretty untactful persuasion on her roommate, Anna.

Anna was a shy, self-conscious Catholic girl with curly strawberry-blonde hair and a sweet personality. She had a cute face and a somewhat plump body that Jewels commented about far too often.

What bothered me even more than Jewels's treatment of poor Anna was the way she talked about my roommate, Payton. Just because Payton was black, Jewels had told me I should request a different roommate, claiming it might affect my ability to get into a good sorority. Jewels's prejudiced remarks, both in front of Payton and behind her back, made me want to yell at her or ignore her. But I knew the Lord wanted me to love her, and I was doing my best to try.

"So, where can I get some nourishment at this hour?" I asked, noticing that my bedside clock said it was almost five.

"Vending machine's down the hall," Payton whispered with a yawn.

I grabbed three quarters out of my jeans pocket, put on my gym clothes, and walked to the vending machine. When I got there I noticed that it only offered sodas, and they cost a dollar.

"What a rip-off!" I started to head back to my room for another quarter, then decided to continue on to the gym to start my early practice.

The halls were quiet, everyone else still sleeping. I envied them in a way. But I knew it would take extra effort to make the University of Georgia gymnastics team, and I was determined to do whatever it took, even if that meant starting practice before anyone else was up.

As I approached the gym, I noticed the door was ajar and lights were on inside. I peeked in.

Someone else had beat me to an early start! I checked my watch. It wasn't even five-thirty.

I stood in the doorway and watched the girl work the parallel bars. She was awesome! Her routine looked flawless. Every move was filled with grace and confidence.

When she dismounted, landing perfectly, I could not believe my eyes. It was my favorite gymnast, Nadia Rhodenhauser. For years I had watched her compete nationally. I knew she was a college freshman, like me, but I didn't know she'd decided to go to the University of Georgia.

She looked shorter in person, even shorter than I, and I was five-feet-five. She probably wore a size three. Seeing her in her Olympics leotard made me long for the day I would wear one just like it.

Nadia was the best gymnast in the nation during eleventh grade, winning the gold medal at the Olympics. In her senior year she won the silver, and Marci Lotts, a girl I'd heard was coming to UG, snagged the gold.

"Are you just going to gawk, or do you want to come in and practice?" Nadia asked with a grin.

"Oh," I said, embarrassed that she'd caught me staring. "I came to work out. I just didn't want to disturb you."

She wiped her face with a towel from her gym bag and reached out to shake my hand. "Hi. I'm Nadia Rhodenhauser."

"I know," I said. "I've watched you for years. When you won the gold medal in the Olympics, I felt like it was my medal, too, in a way."

Nadia chuckled. Her eyes were the prettiest blue I'd ever

15

seen. She'd pulled her curly blonde hair into a ponytail, but most of it had escaped after her vigorous workout. "What's your name?" she asked.

"Laurel Shadrach."

"That sounds familiar."

"I've been in gymnastics since I was in the fourth grade," I said, excited that she might have heard of me. "I went to state competitions with Rockdale Gym and was captain of the Salem High School team."

"I remember you now," she said. "I went to see you at the regionals last year, but you weren't there."

I rolled my eyes. "I sprained my ankle two weeks before the meet!"

"How awful," she said, her eyes soft with compassion. "Are you planning to try out for the team here?"

"I'm hoping to walk on and maybe get a scholarship next year."

"That's great."

Suddenly I wondered if I'd made the right decision. I knew I was nowhere near as good as Nadia Rhodenhauser. How could I compete with her for a spot on the team? Still, if I did make it, what a dream come true that would be!

"Hey, you want a sports drink?" she asked, walking to a vending machine in the corner.

"Sure do," I said, noticing all the nutritious snacks and drinks for sale. "But I've only got seventy-five cents on me."

"No problem," she said. "My treat." She stuffed some change into the machine, and out popped two bottles. She handed one to me.

"I'll buy next time," I offered.

"You've got a deal," she replied.

We sat on a mat to quench our thirst. "What time does the gym open?" I asked.

"Six," she said. "But I get here at four. The janitor lets me in."

I almost choked on my drink. I'd never gotten up before 4 A.M. in my life! "I heard you were going to UCLA," I said.

Nadia smiled. "You really have followed my career." She took a sip. "I did plan on UCLA originally. Most of the girls I've worked with are going there. But Coach Burrows kept trying to recruit me. So, just to be different, I decided to come here."

She finished her last gulp and asked if I'd spot her on the mats. I agreed without hesitation.

She did a tumbling routine that left me breathless and amazed. Her talent was even more impressive in person than on TV.

"Wow," I said. "I still can't believe you're . . . here. And that I'm . . . talking to you." I was tripping all over my words like a groupie. She may not have been a big celebrity to most people, but there wasn't a movie star on the planet I would rather have met.

"I'm just another college freshman like you," she said.

"But you're so . . . good."

"You can be as good as I am," she assured me. "You just have to believe it . . . and practice."

Her words made me realize I hadn't even started working out yet. I began my stretching exercises.

"I didn't want to compete with my former teammates anyway," Nadia confided as she stretched along with me. "They stabbed me in the back."

"What did they do?"

"Two of the girls I worked out with for years were jealous of my boyfriend," she began. "So they made up stories, telling him I was seeing another guy on our gymnastics team. They even went so far as to send him a picture of me kissing the guy."

"How did they get that?"

"After a meet, I gave the guy a congratulations kiss. I tried to explain that to my boyfriend, but he didn't want to hear me out. He apologized later, but when I realized he couldn't trust me, I lost interest in him. I couldn't get close with my girlfriends after that."

Her story reminded me so much of what Brittany and Branson had done to me. I opened up and told her all the details of my senior year fiasco.

"So, when your boyfriend cheated on you, did you get a new one?" she asked.

"Sure did." I giggled. "I dated a Christian guy named Foster for a while."

"Wait a minute," she said, a smile tugging at her lips. "Are you a Christian?"

"Yes," I said. "Are you?"

"Yes!" She wrapped her arms around me and gave me a tight hug. "It's so great to meet a sister in the Lord."

I had heard Nadia give credit to God after a televised meet, and I'd read her testimony in *Gymnastics World*. But I was happy to confirm that her beliefs were real.

"So, are you still seeing that Christian guy?" she asked.

"No," I admitted.

"How come?"

I took a deep breath. For some reason, it felt perfectly natural to share all the secrets of my past with this girl. "I left my first boyfriend because he pressured me to have sex with him, and it really turned me off. But for some reason, when I found a guy who didn't pressure me, I wanted to jump his bones. It was the craziest thing."

"I understand," she said with a nod.

When I started telling Nadia about the shooting that happened at my school, she said she'd heard about it on the news.

"Well," I said, "my brother was the main target, and the shooter held me at gunpoint too."

She gasped.

"In a way, it turned out to be a good thing."

"How?"

"When I thought my life might be over, I figured out

what I really wanted," I told her. "In that moment I realized that Foster didn't have my heart. I was still in love with my ex-boyfriend, Branson."

"Did you get back together with him?" Nadia asked.

"Not right away. I'd already promised Foster I'd go to the prom with him. But at the dance, Branson saw me with him, and he lost it. He had too much to drink and went joyriding with his best friend, Bo. Their car went over a cliff and Bo became paralyzed."

"Oh, no!" she cried, her eyes wide.

"That actually turned out to be kind of a good thing too. Bo came to know Christ because of that ordeal."

"Wow," she whispered. "I thought my high school years were crazy, just going from fifth to first to second in gymnastics."

"I wish that was my only problem." I laughed. "I don't even know if I'm going to make the team here."

She smiled. "I'm going to pray that you do."

"Really?" I squealed. "That'd be great!"

"I'd also like to help you out with some gymnastics tips I've learned," she told me. She nodded at the balance beam. "How are you on the beam?"

"It's my favorite apparatus," I said.

"Great," she said. "Show me what you've got."

I approached the beam and gave it my best shot. When I dismounted, Nadia Rhodenhauser actually applauded me.

As she showed me some moves on the vault, we chatted some more. She told me she was an only child. Her mother had worked three jobs for as long as Nadia could remember, since her dad had walked out on them shortly after Nadia was born.

When she was sixteen, her dad suddenly came back into her life. At first she was reluctant to trust him, but he showed up at every meet she'd had over the last two years, and gradually a bond developed between them.

Her parents fought constantly whenever they were

around each other. Nadia had figured she was the reason they'd broken up, so she tried really hard to bring them back together. But nothing worked.

"Coach Gailey and his wife were my saving grace," Nadia told me as we rested between routines. "They introduced me to Jesus Christ, and they provided me with a stability I never knew at home."

At Nadia's urging, we worked on a complex tumbling trick. Finally I collapsed on the mat, unable to move. Nadia performed a routine on the uneven bars and gave me a grin.

"Now I know why I'm not as good as you," I teased.

"You can be," she said, "if you really want it."

"I do," I assured her.

"Then keep practicing," she advised.

"Want to work out together tomorrow?" I asked.

"Sure," she said. "Four o'clock?"

I gulped. Then I said, "I'll be here."

We hugged, then went our separate ways to get ready for class.

———————

When I walked back into the dorm room, Payton was standing there, dripping wet, a towel wrapped around her. Her caramel-colored skin glowed, and her curly, shoulder-length brown hair sparkled with water droplets. "Where have you been?" she asked.

"Practicing," I reminded her as I went to the closet to pick out clothes for the day.

"You're sweaty," she said. "You want some water?" She strode to the refrigerator. When she opened the door, I saw a row of bottled water on the shelf.

"Where'd you get that?" I asked as she pulled one out.

"I had a talk with Jewels this morning. She admitted to stealing all our drinks, and since she had tons of water in her fridge, I made her give me half." She opened the bottle and handed it to me.

"Thanks for being such a good roommate," I said after taking a long drink.

"No biggie."

"No, I really appreciate it."

"I'm going to go get dressed," she said.

When she went into the bathroom, I dropped to my knees on the hardwood floor. *Lord, I'm worried about my future. I feel so frail. I need Your strength, Your power, Your guidance. Help me see what I need to do. I want to go forward and not look back. Take over my thoughts and make them positive, fresh, and righteous. Guide my actions. Make me stand for You in all I say and do, and help me to be an example for those who are trying to live Your way. Help me to lead people to You.*

My knees started to hurt, and I considered ending my prayer there. Instead I reached for a pillow, placed it under my knees, and continued.

Thank You for Payton. And for Jewels and Anna. I pray for Nadia and for my parents. I pray for Branson and Foster too. When I start acting more like a person of the world than a child of Yours, help me get back to putting You first. Thank You for showing me what I've done wrong and what I did that was right. I'm looking forward to being a freshman here at the University of Georgia. I'm no longer recapping senior year.

wishing
for harmony

"Y ou shouldn't have worn that," Jewels said to me at our first day of sorority rush.

I looked down at my floral print dress. I had on a Ralph Lauren outfit I'd bought only two years ago. I thought it looked nice on me—not too tight but not old-fashioned. The fuchsia and pink flowers set off my brown eyes and long light-brown hair nicely, in my opinion. But Jewels said the colors made my skin look too red, like I was breaking out in hives or something.

Jewels had made poor Anna, her roommate, change five times before she approved of her outfit. I never saw any of the options; I just heard the two girls bickering through the bathroom door. When I did see Anna, her dress was adorable. The short-sleeved brown suit complemented her larger frame. And pinning her curly strawberry-blonde hair up with bobby pins gave her a classy look.

Jewels wore a sky-blue dress that looked great with the

red hair that flowed down her back. Her super-short skirt showed off her shapely legs. She'd told me once that she took dance lessons for fifteen years. It certainly showed. I wished my years in gymnastics had carved my body so well.

Jewels strutted down the sidewalk like a peacock. Anna and I followed her to the coliseum, along with hundreds of other freshman girls hoping to find a sorority home.

Though I didn't want to admit it, I started to feel self-conscious about my outfit. Jewels's comment about my skin looking like hives weighed heavily on my mind. As we walked through the oak double doors of the coliseum, I actually started scratching.

Jewels and Anna and I took seats in the middle row on the left side of the coliseum. I looked over at Jewels and whispered, "I think my outfit is cute."

"So do I," she said, apparently forgetting what she had told me earlier. "You look great," she added in a sincere tone.

Her assurance made me feel more confident. I hated that her opinion meant so much to me, but Jewels seemed to know what the sororities were looking for. Her sister, Julie Anne, was president of the Alpha Gamma Delta sorority, which I'd heard was the best one on campus.

At Jewels's prodding, I had skipped my early morning gymnastics practice so I'd be fresh and well rested for my sorority appearances. I felt guilty about breaking my promise to Nadia, and I wondered how the missed practice would affect my athletic abilities. But getting into a good sorority was almost as important to me as gymnastics.

As we waited for the program to begin, I reread the pamphlet I'd received from the student affairs office about the sorority selection process. Basically, there were three rounds to go through. In round one, we'd visit all the sororities to get an overall feel for what they were about and decide which ones we wanted to join. It was important to make a good impression so the houses we liked would invite us back. According to the pamphlet, it would take two days for us to visit every sorority house on campus.

A few days after the end of round one, all prospective members would receive a list of the houses they were welcome to visit again. I'd heard that some girls didn't get any invitations to return, while others were asked by so many sororities they had to choose which ones to go back to, as there was a maximum number allowed for the second round.

While the first round allowed up to thirty minutes per visit, each second-round visit lasted one hour. It involved more meeting and greeting and hopefully making more positive impressions. Following these visits, each girl would submit her top three choices to student affairs. At the same time, each sorority sent in a list of the girls they wanted.

In the last round, the school computer matched everyone up, and each student would be given a card with the names of all the girls who'd been accepted into that sorority.

On pledge night the girls would go to their new sorority houses. The brochure indicated that this was a grand celebration. I looked at the photo showing a group of attractive girls hugging and celebrating in front of their sorority house. As I imagined myself in that scene, hope filled my heart.

My musings were cut short when a short man stood on the raised stage and tapped the microphone, causing feedback that made everyone wince. "Good morning, ladies," he said in a high-pitched voice, having assured himself that the mike was working. "I am Walt Kimbrough, vice president of student affairs." We gave him a polite round of applause.

"I am pleased to announce that there are three thousand freshmen women enrolled here this year. One of the largest classes we've ever had." This time we applauded more enthusiastically.

"Every one of you young ladies is deserving of a sorority, and I am certain you would each be a tremendous benefit. However, about one-third of you won't make it into one. And although being in a sorority is a fun and exciting experience, we have lots of other activities you can be involved in as well."

I knew Mr. Kimbrough had a point. I really wanted to make it into Alpha Gamma Delta. But every girl there had her hopes, and not everyone's dreams would come true. I prayed that God would give me peace, no matter what happened. Even if I didn't get into any sorority, my joy was in Christ, not the things of the world.

After Mr. Kimbrough's speech, a bunch of buses took us all to the beautiful sorority houses on Milledge Avenue. I'd seen them when I first came on campus, when I was deciding whether or not to go to Georgia. They were breathtaking. Row after row of large, new buildings with lush green lawns perfectly manicured, bright flowers popping up everywhere.

"Come on, Laurel," Jewels said in a bossy voice. "We're going straight to the Alpha Gamma Delta house. I want to be the first person they see."

"Why?" Anna asked.

Jewels rolled her eyes. "Because they're the best, of course."

"You're just saying that because your sister's the president of that sorority," I said.

Jewels crossed her arms across her chest. "That's one reason they're the best!"

"You go ahead," I said. "I'm just going to start with the first one on the block and work my way up. Whichever ones I don't hit today I'll get to tomorrow."

Her mouth dropped open and her eyebrows rose, like she thought my idea was totally stupid.

"I'm going to stick with Laurel," Anna announced.

Jewels took several frustrated breaths. Finally she said, "No one should go up to a sorority house alone. It's a sign that they're unfriendly. Guess I'll just stick with you guys."

Anna gave me a look that told me she wished Jewels would have gone on without us. I entertained the same thought for a minute.

We started for the Tri Delta house. A sorority member came out and greeted us, found out our names, then introduced us to our guide, Opal. We toured the sorority house and met several members, who were all really friendly. We enjoyed some cheese, crackers, cookies, and punch, chatting with people until we felt we'd learned what we needed to know.

"This is going to take a long time," Anna said as we walked back outside.

"Just keep smiling," Jewels said, hurrying toward the next house.

I grinned from ear to ear just because Jewels told me to. "Why should we keep smiling?"

"Opal is grading us," she said as we strolled down the sidewalk.

"What do you mean?" I asked.

"How do you think they narrow down who they want?"

"I thought they weren't supposed to do any narrowing until the second round," Anna said.

"Oh, Anna, you know nothing about this," Jewels said. "It's a good thing you've got me. Now, stop walking with your shoulders hunched over. Stand up straighter. You're making me look bad."

Anna looked like she was about to cry. I felt bad for her. Jewels didn't have to hurt her feelings like that. But I didn't say anything. They were roommates. I figured it was best if I stayed out of their little spats.

We visited ten sorority houses that day. By five o'clock my feet were killing me and I suggested we call it quits.

Jewels fussed all the way home. "I can't believe we didn't see the Alpha Gams today. We have got to go to their house first tomorrow, no matter what."

Part of me wanted to tell her to hush up already. But to keep the peace, I just let her get tired of hearing herself. Anna and I finally consented that our first stop the next day would be the Alpha Gamma Delta house.

I hadn't been particularly impressed by any of the places I'd been that day. And from the way Jewels had raved about the Alpha Gams, I was actually looking forward to seeing what they were about. Besides, that had been my mother's sorority, and I knew it would make her proud if I became an Alpha Gam too.

When I got back to my room, I found it empty. I was kind of relieved. I really liked my roommate, but after being surrounded by girls all day, being alone was a blessing.

I tossed my heavy bag of sorority flyers into the corner chair and put on my favorite country western CD. I turned the volume up, higher than I knew Payton would have liked. Then I sank into the chair, propped my feet up, and just enjoyed my space.

As promised, Alpha Gamma Delta was our first stop the next day. It was a two-story building made of taupe stucco, with little windows near the ground that indicated it had a basement. Four wicker rocking chairs sat on the porch surrounded by four big columns. I couldn't wait to go in.

As I stood on the lawn gaping at the sorority house, I heard a voice call out, "Laurel Shadrach!"

I turned around and saw a brunette girl about my height headed toward me. I immediately recognized her as the Alpha Gamma Delta pledge master, whom I'd met at the block party. Her sweet, welcoming spirit had made my heart soar. Even though we were only in round one of the pledge process, and we had four more days left, none of the other houses had made me feel so at home.

"Liza, right?" I guessed.

"Yeah!" Her face lit up. "I was praying I'd get to show you around."

"Really?" I asked, amazed. "You were praying about me?"

"I checked on your background a little, and it turns out

27

we have a lot in common. I used to live in Conway, Arkansas."

"No way!" I cried. I'd grown up in Conway and moved to Georgia just before high school.

"Our grandmothers were sorority sisters at the University of Arkansas," Liza continued. "They were Alpha Gams there too!"

"You're kidding." I was thrilled that I had so much in common with this nice girl.

Liza grinned. "With all the things your mom and your grandmother told me about you, I'm sure you won't have any problem getting in here."

A sour thought suddenly hit me. "I don't want to get into Alpha Gamma Delta just because of my 'connections.' I want to make it on my own."

Liza laughed. "That makes me even more excited about having you here." She put her arm around my shoulders and led me into the beautiful house. The hardwood floors, spiral staircase, and formal living and dining room areas made me feel like I had stepped into a miniature castle. Everything was decorated in burgundy and forest green, the Alpha Gam colors.

"Your mom said our grandmothers were really good friends back in their college days," Liza said. "Your grandma was a year older than mine, and they had a lot of fun together."

"And you're a year older than I!" I exclaimed.

"That's right!"

I was amazed at the similarities in our lives.

"Even though I'm just a sophomore," Liza said, "a lot of the older gals here really like me. And I plan to use my favor to get you in here . . . and not just because your mom asked me to. So, why don't you let me introduce you to some folks around here? This really is the best sorority on campus."

The tour was only supposed to last for thirty minutes, but Liza showed me around for almost an hour and a half. Jewels tagged along the whole time.

When I finally said good-bye to Liza, and Jewels and I stepped outside, I started to wonder what had happened to Anna.

"It's about time," Anna hollered from across the street. "I went to two other houses while you were in there."

"That's not good," Jewels whispered to me as Anna waited for traffic to clear so she could cross over to us.

"It would be nice if we all ended up in the same sorority," I said.

Just as Anna joined us, a pretty girl with short red hair came out the front door of the Alpha Gamma Delta house and squealed at Jewels. When the girls hugged each other, I saw a definite family resemblance and figured this must be Julie Anne, the big sister Jewels had bragged about so much.

My suspicions were confirmed when Jewels introduced us.

"Hey, I've heard a lot about you from Liza," Julie Anne said to me. "She thinks very highly of you."

"Really?" I said, thrilled that the pledge master had mentioned me.

"You know," she said, leaning in close and speaking softly, "as president of the Alpha Gams, I pull a lot of weight when it comes to deciding who gets in and who doesn't."

My heart skipped a beat.

"I definitely plan on putting in a good word for you."

Having the president of the sorority talk to me with such interest made me feel really special. But the glare in Jewels's eyes filled me with apprehension. And Anna's sad expression made me wish she hadn't heard the glowing words being said about me.

"There are going to be three frat parties tonight," Julie Anne informed us. "Get to the KA party. A lot of the Alpha Gams will be there, so you'll get a chance to meet more of us."

"Sounds like fun," I said. "Thanks."

Julie Anne gave me a conspiratorial grin. "You rated really high today. So if you come to the Kappa Alpha party tonight, you can suck up a little bit. Hand out a compliment here and there." She winked at Jewels. "Tell her how it's done."

"Will do," Jewels agreed, not sounding particularly excited about it.

"I've got to go back in. Wouldn't want it to look like I'm showing favoritism!" Julie Anne winked at us and headed back to the house.

"Looks like you're going to get into Alpha Gamma Delta for sure," Anna said to Jewels as we walked to the next house.

"Yeah, probably," Jewels grumbled.

"What's wrong?" I asked, trying to draw her out.

She hesitated. "I don't want my sister to just write my ticket." She looked up at me. "You know what I mean?"

I knew exactly what she meant. "But you do want to get in, right?"

"Of course I do."

"Well, then, tell me what we need to do at that party tonight."

She smiled. We were finally connecting.

"Hey, I want to get in too," Anna whined, stepping between us.

"Then why did you leave the tour?" I asked.

Anna looked at the ground. "Nobody was really talking to me, and my guide escorted me out pretty quick. I didn't even get to tell you guys I was leaving. So I just went to some other houses."

"That's probably for the best," Jewels said. "I didn't want to say anything earlier, but you're not really Alpha Gam material."

Anna's head dropped. The rude words had cut her deeply. Suddenly the connection I'd felt with Jewels died. Her insensitive manner made me not want to be around her at all.

"You two can go to more houses if you want," Jewels

said, "but I'm worn out. I'm going to go home and rest up before the party."

Jewels took off without another word. I wanted to cheer Anna up but didn't know what to say.

Anna and I visited a couple of other houses, and then we returned to the dorm too.

When I walked into my room, Payton was listening to rap music and painting her toenails. I couldn't stand rap music. "Could you please turn that down?"

"Why?" she said in a snotty way. "It's not that loud."

"It's irritating to me," I said.

She snorted. "It's better than that country stuff you listen to."

"Yeah, well, when you ask me to turn it down, I do. So have some common courtesy, OK?"

"Well, isn't that the pot calling the kettle black," she said.

"Look, Payton, I'm really tired. I don't want to fuss with you."

"Then don't," she replied as she went back to painting her toenails.

I walked over to her side of the room and turned off her stereo.

"Don't touch my stuff," she growled, standing.

I stood my ground. Her attitude didn't scare me.

We yelled at each other for a few minutes, and Payton finally stormed off into the bathroom and slammed the door.

I immediately regretted my harsh words. I dropped down on my knees.

Lord, please help us. I know we have our differences. Help us find some middle ground. Right now I think our only common thread is You.

Exhausted from my long day of walking, I crawled onto the bed and continued my prayer.

About thirty minutes later Payton came back from the bathroom. "I'm sorry," she said in a soft voice. "I should have turned down my music when you asked me to."

"I forgive you," I said right away.

"Want to go down to the café and get something to eat?"

I smiled. "That sounds good," I said, inwardly thanking my heavenly Father. He had changed Payton's spirit. And mine too. I was grateful for the power of prayer.

As we walked to the café, we talked about our argument. We both admitted it was stupid to fight about something so unimportant.

"I'm glad we're able to laugh this off," I said as we reached the cafeteria building. "I don't want any tension between us."

"Me neither," she said, heading for the buffet line.

"You know, while you were in the bathroom, I was praying that God—"

"I was praying too," she said.

"Well, He sure answers quick sometimes."

"He sure does," she said, and we hugged each other.

"You look pretty with your hair up like that," Payton said to me as I stared at my reflection in the mirror.

Payton had never seen my hair pulled up in a ponytail since I usually wore it down and straight. But I wanted to do something special to go with my red dress, which was fitted at the waist and flared out at the bottom. Black sandals and a matching purse completed the look nicely, I thought.

I thanked her for the compliment, then added, "You look nice too." She wore an adorable casual outfit of blue jeans and a sassy top.

My roommate and I were both getting ready for a party, but we were each planning to attend a different one. I was going to the KA frat party to meet more Alpha Gams. Payton was going to a party sponsored by the Student Government Association for African-American students.

As I checked out my appearance in the mirror, all I could think about was the party I'd gone to with my high school girlfriends Brittany and Meagan, where we ended up being the entertainment for a bunch of drunk fraternity guys. I hoped this party wouldn't turn out like that one.

I chose a dainty fake-diamond bracelet to wear with my red dress, but I dropped it twice trying to put it on. Payton shook her head and offered to help me with the latch.

"Guess I'm pretty nervous," I admitted.

My parents and my brothers had always urged me to stay away from parties . . . except Lance, my middle brother. He was a party guy. He also had a problem with alcohol and gambling. Not the kind of lifestyle I wanted to emulate.

I wanted to become an Alpha Gamma Delta but at what cost? My mom had pledged a long time ago, and my grand-mother even longer. Things were probably a lot different back then.

I pulled my hair down in one quick yank of the scrunchie. "I'm not going."

"What do you mean?" Payton asked. "You were all excit-ed a minute ago."

I flopped down onto the bed. "You go on to your party. I'll be fine. I just kind of feel like Christians shouldn't."

"Shouldn't what? Party?"

"Yeah," I said, my convictions growing the more I thought about it. "Parties usually involve alcohol and danc-ing real close and loud music, all in the dark. Christians are supposed to walk in the light."

Payton sat on the bed beside me. "I didn't realize you felt that way."

"Neither did I," I said, "till just now."

Payton stood. "If you don't think you should go, then you shouldn't. But I believe I can be a light in the darkness. I mean, I'm not going there to witness to anybody," she ad-mitted. "But I can have a good time without losing my faith."

I looked up at my roommate. "Are you saying you think I should go to my party too?"

"If you really think God is telling you to stay home, then that's what you should do. But are you sure you're hearing right? I know what happened to you at that frat party over the summer. Maybe you're just afraid, and saying that God doesn't want you to party makes everything sound all spiritual."

I didn't know what to say.

"Laurel, the only way to handle your fears is to face them. You won't be going alone. You'll have those crazy girls on the other side of the wall with you. As long as Jewels isn't planning to stay all night or anything—"

"I know she's not," I said, "because she said pledges aren't supposed to stay out late."

"Well, there you go." She laughed. "You might beat me home because I'm not pledging anything."

The door that led to the bathroom we shared with Jewels and Anna bumped, and the knob jiggled. "Why is this door locked?" Jewels complained from the other side.

"I'm out of here," Payton said, standing. "I don't even want to talk to that girl."

"Be careful," I called out to my roommate before she shut the door to the hall.

"Are you ready, Laurel?" Jewels asked through the closed door.

I unlocked the door, and Jewels barged in wearing cream-colored silk pants and a pale pink button-down blouse. Before I could tell her how cute she looked, she said, "Wow! That dress is a killer. I wish I had one just like it."

As we drove to the Kappa Alpha house, I thought about Payton's words. I sure hoped she was right. I didn't want to walk in fear. Maybe I did need to test myself. My faith should be bigger than my circumstances.

On the other hand, I still believed that Christians shouldn't put themselves in compromising positions where they knew they would be tempted.

I sat in the backseat of Jewels's Mustang convertible and looked up at the stars, trying to seek guidance. But Jewels's shrill voice kept interrupting my meditation.

"You should prepare yourself for the probability that you won't make it into a sorority," she was telling Anna. "If you didn't get any warm, fuzzy feelings from anyone earlier today, then probably no one's going to want you."

Jewels's logic was way off. Many times, I'd heard, sororities didn't want to let a girl know they were considering her until they were finished rating her. Today had only been the first round. But I could tell from her silence that Anna was buying what Jewels was selling.

I wanted to say something but decided to wait. It was too hard making my voice heard over the Mustang's engine and the breeze blowing over the windshield.

When we pulled up to the frat house, the first thing I noticed was that there were no cars in the parking lot and no people milling around. "Are you sure this is where they're having the party?" I asked.

"We're just early," Jewels stated confidently as she strode up the walkway. "It's only nine o'clock. Things won't get cranking till about ten."

"Maybe we should come back later," Anna suggested.

"There's nothing wrong with being early," Jewels said. "It'll work in our favor. Proves we're really interested."

"I don't like being the first one to arrive at a party," I said, "unless I know most of the people there."

Jewels rolled her eyes at both of us. "I'm sure some of the sorority girls are in there already."

"Then where are their cars?" I asked.

"They probably walked," Jewels huffed. "Why are you making such a big deal?"

Against my better judgment I followed Jewels to the front door, where she rang the doorbell. We were greeted by two upperclassmen who probably weighed two hundred pounds each. Both of them reeked of alcohol. One picked Jewels up and grabbed her bottom. When he put her down, she punched him in the shoulder. He laughed like a buffoon.

The second guy stared at me like I was his dinner. "Tonight," he said to me, "I'm gonna have my way with you."

"I don't think so," I said, taking a step back. I peeked around the guy's hefty arm and saw the place was full of guys. Not a single girl.

"I'm not going in there," I whispered to Anna, turning around.

Before I could take two steps, the big upperclassman grabbed my arm and jerked me inside. "Now, wait a minute, baby. There is definitely going to be a party here tonight. Crank up the music, Scooter!"

"Please let go of my arm," I said, starting to feel panicked. When the guy didn't release me, I repeated my request, louder, and without the *please*.

The guy let go of my arm, but he grabbed my behind with both hands and squeezed me close to him. I struggled to get out of his grasp.

I heard a loud smack and my captor suddenly let me go. He reeled away and went sprawling onto the floor. When I realized he'd been socked in the mouth, I turned to see who'd rescued me. I couldn't believe my eyes.

"Branson!"

He stood there, flushed, rubbing his knuckles on the red-and-white barbecue apron tied around his waist. That gorgeous blond-haired stud still made my heart race, even though we were no longer together. His bright blue eyes made me want to take him in my arms and never let him go.

The big guy on the floor yelled, "You're finished, Price. You're never gonna make this fraternity. Get your things and go."

Branson untied the apron and threw it on the angry upperclassman. "Suits me just fine, Craig. You guys are a bunch of wimps anyway."

Before I could thank Branson for coming to my rescue, a guy in a white cotton shirt, khaki pants, and a red-and-black tie came up to us. "Come on," he said, nodding to a couple of his friends, "get this loser out of here." It took three guys to escort my assailant out of the room, struggling and hollering obscenities the whole way.

The newcomer turned to us. "I'm Bill," he said. "I'm the president of this fraternity, and I want to tell you ladies how sorry I am for Craig's behavior."

I nodded in appreciation of his concern. Jewels batted her eyes at him, practically flirting with the guy. Anna headed quietly for the refreshments table.

Bill slapped Branson on the back. "Hey, that was impressive. I like seeing a guy stand up for a lady like that. We could use someone like you around here."

Branson beamed. "Thanks," he said.

Bill placed his arm around Branson, and they walked toward the crowd of guys who'd been watching from a distance. They all cheered, and Branson soaked up the attention like a dried-up sponge.

My heart cheered for him too. He had risked his opportunity to be in the fraternity for me. Did that mean we had a chance of being together again? Was this the start of something new and even better for the two of us?

Suddenly I felt someone bump me hard in the arm. I turned, ready to scream for Branson's help, but just saw Jewels and Anna standing there.

"Hello," Jewels said in an irritated voice, nodding at the two cups Anna was holding. "We brought you some punch."

"Oh," I said. "I'm sorry." I felt terrible for paying so much attention to Branson that I'd totally neglected my girlfriends. "Thanks, Anna."

As I took a sip of the refreshing drink, I wondered if I should wait for Branson to come to me or make the first move. I had to do something. I couldn't let this opportunity pass by. Deep in my heart I wished we were back together again. I wanted things to work out for us. I was wishing for harmony.

giving
my pledge

that ex-boyfriend of yours is so cute," Jewels said. "Now, tell me again, why is he your *ex*-boyfriend?"

As Branson walked away to brag to his friends about decking Craig, I stood there like I was watching a movie. I wanted to thank him for coming to my rescue, but he hadn't even turned to look at me to make sure I was OK. He was apparently more excited about winning brownie points with the fraternity than he was about me.

I stepped a few feet away from Jewels, closer to Branson. I fixed my eyes on him, hoping he'd notice me. He didn't.

"See, now, that's how it's supposed to be," Jewels said, watching Branson as she came up behind me. "Even though he's not officially in the fraternity, he knows he's in! Sororities are the same way. They let you know if they want you so you can want them even more. It's like a game."

I didn't bother responding to her comment.

Anna came up behind Jewels with her lips in a pout.

Jewels pushed her back and told her to go somewhere else. Anna's eyes teared up.

"You're much too sensitive," Jewels said to her. "Sororities want strong, confident women, you know."

Spotting her sister, Julie Anne, entering the house with a group of Alpha Gams, Jewels waved and joined them, forgetting all about me and Anna.

"Are you OK?" Anna asked through her tears. "Did that guy hurt you?"

"No," I said. "But Jewels sure has been hurting you with her remarks, hasn't she?"

Anna shrugged, her tears coming stronger.

"Don't worry about it," I said, putting my arm around her. "I'm sure she didn't mean to be so insensitive."

"Do you think I have a chance of getting into a sorority?" she asked, her lower lip trembling.

I started to tell her that pledging to a sorority wasn't that big a deal. But I could tell it was important to her. Just like gymnastics was important to me.

"Anna, I don't know how this whole thing works. I don't want to give you false hopes. But you shouldn't worry about it. If we don't get into a sorority, it's not going to kill us. We'll just find something else fun to do here."

She sniffed and wiped her cheek with the back of her hand. "Thanks, Laurel."

"You know, it's getting a little crowded in here," I said. "I'm going to go get some water and then we can leave."

"Don't worry about me," she said. "I'll be fine."

As I started toward the kitchen to get a drink, I saw Branson. Two girls stood beside him, batting their eyes and flashing their pearly whites at him. They were cute, but I knew there was no way they could give him what I could, and I didn't mean sex. I meant love. Though I'd tried hard not to love Branson, I had to admit that I did. And I knew I had to tell him that.

I took a deep breath and walked up to him. "Hi, Branson," I said.

The two girls glared at me.

I glared right back. "Now, you girls wouldn't be fooling around with my boyfriend, by any chance, would you?"

"Boyfriend?" one of them huffed, giving Branson a cold look. "You didn't tell me you had a girlfriend."

I slid into his arms and kissed him on the cheek.

The first girl stormed off. The second one said in a huff, "Well, I guess you won't need my number after all." Then she followed her friend out of the room.

I smiled. Branson didn't.

"What was that all about?" he asked. "We're not together anymore."

"Branson," I said, stepping close to him, "I . . . I love you."

He placed his arm on my shoulder. "I love you too," he said softly.

"I know," I said coyly. "I could tell by the way you stopped that guy from disrespecting me."

"I've always cared about you, Laurel," he said. "And I always will." He looked away, and I could sense a *but* coming on.

"I just don't want to be with you anymore. It's taken me weeks to get over you." He removed his arm from my shoulder and stepped back. "I can't go back now. Please respect that, OK?"

"Can't we talk about this?"

One of the KAs swooped up to us. "Hey, man," he said in a slurred voice. "It's not time for serious stuff. This is a party!" He grabbed Branson's arm and pulled him into a train of about thirty guys, some with sheets wrapped around their bodies, singing a bawdy song as they wove through the crowded fraternity house.

I stood there alone and watched the toga train, trying to pull myself together.

So, Branson said we're through. But he hadn't rescued me that evening just because he wanted to impress his friends. He had to care about me to jump in like he did.

Jewels dashed up to me. "Come on, let's go."

I didn't know why she was in such a hurry to leave, but I suddenly wanted to get out of there too. I knew Branson would look for me sooner or later and wonder where I'd gone. Well, if he wanted to play hard to get, fine. I knew he loved me as much as I loved him, and I was determined to make him see that. It might take some time, but I was in it for the long haul.

"What about Anna?" I said.

"She left a long time ago," Jewels told me.

"Alone?" I asked, worried about her.

"I guess so," Jewels said, apparently unconcerned.

Jewels babbled about nothing all the way back to the dorm. I ignored her, listening instead to an inner argument going on inside my heart.

Why are you trying so hard to hang on to Branson? one voice said. *He told you he doesn't want to go out with you.*

I don't want to give him up, the other voice whined.

That jerk cheated on you, the practical voice reminded me. *He tried to force you to have sex with him. He almost got AIDS. He treats you like garbage. Is that the kind of relationship you want to keep pushing for?*

But maybe there's a better guy inside, my romantic side suggested. *One who's a Christian and lives like one.*

I think you need to rethink this whole thing.

I was so confused I didn't know what to think.

"Oh, my gosh," Jewels squealed, staring at the invitation list Mr. Kimbrough had handed out. "Your list is just like mine."

We stood in the student affairs courtyard with all the other girls going through the sorority selection process. The top twelve sororities had invited both Jewels and me to come back for round two. "And look, Alpha Gam is on top of both of our lists."

We grabbed each other and jumped up and down together. Then I saw Anna, who stood a few feet away from us, staring at her list. She was biting her trembling lower lip.

Jewels started toward her. Figuring she would probably say something insulting, I grabbed her arm. "Let me talk to her."

"You should prepare her," she whispered. "I'm sure her list doesn't look like ours."

"Jewels, that's enough already."

"Fine. Say whatever you want to her. But don't spend too much time. We've got to go back and visit all these places as soon as possible. I'm going to freshen up. Then we can go to Alpha Gam together."

"We'll see," I said.

Jewels rolled her eyes and took off toward the dorm. As I walked over to Anna, I pulled a tissue out of my purse.

"Thanks," she whispered, taking the tissue from me. "Look at this." She showed me her list.

It was far from impressive. I didn't even recognize some of the sororities on her list. But at least she'd been invited back to some. That was a blessing. I could tell from the whispered conversations buzzing around me that some of the girls hadn't been invited back to any of the sororities. I tried to comfort Anna with that observation, but it didn't make her happy.

"None of these sororities are the popular ones."

"That's all right," I assured her. "Once you get into one of these, you can make it popular."

"How can I do that when I'm not popular myself?"

"Don't talk like that."

"Laurel, I'm not stupid. I know why the good sororities don't want me. Jewels helped me see it. I should have listened. I don't know why I had any hopes for Alpha Gamma Delta. I was only kidding myself." She rushed away.

Silently I asked the Lord for guidance. I wanted to do something to relieve Anna's pain.

Within my spirit, I heard the Lord reply, *Just keep encouraging her. Let her know she has your support.*

I promised myself I would do that the next time I saw her.

I hurried to the dorm, and as soon as Jewels and I made ourselves presentable, we headed to the Alpha Gamma Delta house for round two, which was Colors Day. All the sororities had their colors on display. Alpha Gam's house was decorated in burgundy and forest green, and all the sorority sisters were wearing those colors. Even the refreshment table had burgundy and green napkins, plates, and cups.

Colors Day, we'd been told, meant showing lots of spirit and having lots of fun. That sounded good to me! But as soon as Jewels and I entered the sorority building, I noticed the two girls I'd seen with Branson at the frat party. They were sipping red punch and giggling, and the sound of their laughter made my skin crawl.

One of them noticed me, whispered to her friend, and then they both smiled sweetly at me. I put on a pleasant face and nodded back at them.

I glanced over my shoulder and saw Jewels. She was chatting with a group of Alpha Gams, glowing with confidence. Something in me clicked and I stepped up to the plate. I went around reintroducing myself to the sorority girls and asking them if they had any questions about me. Several said they were really impressed with my assertiveness.

I helped myself to the generous spread of appetizers. Everything was scrumptious. I especially liked the meatballs and the fruit with chocolate fondue dip.

The sorority girls performed a skit about sisterhood that was hysterical. But it also had a great message. After spending the day with them, I knew without a doubt this was where I wanted to be.

The next day, the sororities handed out another list. This one was much shorter than the first one. But Jewels and I had again been accepted by all of our top choices.

Anna's list was even shorter than ours. Only one place had invited her back to visit. "I should just quit trying," she muttered. "Why go through all the hassle?"

"Don't give up," I told her. "Maybe this is the right place for you."

"Maybe," she mumbled.

"Look at it this way," I said with a grin. "At least you don't have to agonize over which ones to spend the most time at."

Anna smiled, and I prayed with her for all three of us.

As we walked back to the dorm, I said more encouraging things to Anna, trying to lift her up. Jewels said nothing. But by the time we arrived, Anna seemed less distraught. When we went to our separate rooms, she actually smiled at me.

A few minutes later, Jewels and I were in her Mustang, driving to the Alpha Gamma Delta house. "I don't know why you even bother with Anna," she said as she turned a corner.

"How can you say that?" I said, shocked at her rude attitude.

"Just being around her is depressing, and you treat her like a baby. I don't get it."

I wondered if this was the right time for me to witness to Jewels. I had already told her about God and what His Word says about treating our neighbors as ourselves. So I decided to drop another small seed. "It's not just me who cares about Anna. The Holy Spirit wants to love her through me."

"The holy what?" she asked, taking her eyes off the road for a second to frown at me.

"The Holy Spirit is part of the Trinity—God the Father, God the Son, and God the Holy Spirit. The Spirit was given to believers when Jesus Christ ascended into heaven."

"OK," she said, like I'd just told her I still believed in

Santa Claus. "How do you know this Holy Spirit is inside you?"

"I believe it by faith. The Holy Spirit helps me do things that my natural self would just blow off—like this situation with Anna. It would be a lot easier for me to care less about her pain. But the Holy Spirit lets me feel other people's hurts. He enables me to empathize with what they're going through."

"Whatever," she muttered, shaking her head.

"I have a deep desire for everyone in the world to know God," I said, praying that the Holy Spirit would speak to Jewels through my words. "The Lord has a purpose for my life. It's not to fulfill my dreams but to help me win souls for Him."

"My only purpose right now is to become an Alpha Gam," Jewels said.

"Sure, being in a sorority would be great. But if I don't get into Alpha Gam, it's OK because that's not who I am. I'm a child of the King!"

"That's easy for you to say," Jewels commented, speeding a little in a twenty-five-mile-per-hour zone. "You'll probably make it into a great sorority. But Anna needs to come to grips with the fact that her fat self won't get into any sorority."

"If you take pleasure in hurting other people with harsh words," I said, getting upset even though Anna hadn't heard Jewels's mean comment, "there's something wrong with you. I care about Anna and I don't want her to be down. I hope my prayers will help lift her up."

Jewels shook her head as she pulled into the Alpha Gamma Delta parking lot. She didn't seem to totally buy into what I was saying. But that was OK. I just wanted her to hear it. I hoped, someday soon, she would be convinced.

———————————

"So, Shadrach, you decided to join us after all, huh?" Coach Ide, the assistant gymnastics coach, said as I walked into the gym. He was tall and slender. I could tell from the confident way he acted around all the various apparatus that he'd been a dynamite gymnast in his day. His youthful yet mature look made him appear to be in his late twenties.

Official workouts were not scheduled to begin until after school started. But Nadia had suggested I come to the gym and practice as often as I could. If I wanted to make the team, she said, I needed to let the coaches know how dedicated I was.

I'd only missed a few early morning workouts with Nadia, but I still felt rusty. I also felt a little undeserving of practicing in this awesome facility. I had attended a few of the Gym Dawgs gymnastic meets when I was in high school, but as I got out there on the floor, actually mounting the balance beam, touching the uneven bars, stepping onto the perfect mat for the floor routines, I knew I had to make this team.

Since I hadn't heard a final decision yet about my acceptance into the Alpha Gams, I was a little anxious. When I came face-to-face with the head coach, I realized that I needed to put pledging out of my mind and get focused.

Coach Burrows, a curly haired brunette, had been kind enough to see me over the summer, when I'd missed the championships because of a sprained ankle, and I wanted to convince her to let me do a walk-on for gymnastics like Branson was doing for football. She'd been really nice to me that day, but she'd made it clear she couldn't just hand out scholarships on a whim. If I really wanted to be a part of the Georgia team, I'd have to prove I was the best.

"Shadrach," Coach Burrows bellowed as I dismounted from a fairly complicated balance beam routine, "you look sloppy. I've been watching you, and I'm not impressed with what I've seen. You need to show a lot more than that to make this team. Our goal is to win a championship this year. We need athletes who can help us do that. Is that clear?"

"Yes, ma'am," I mumbled. "I understand."

Coach Burrows left my side and joined Coach Ide, who was watching a cute African American girl. She was doing a dance to music, not tumbling or working any apparatus. Though she performed a graceful dance routine, I didn't see what it had to do with gymnastics.

"That's Summer Love," Nadia told me. "She's your competition for the last slot on the team."

When she fell off the balance beam, Coach Burrows praised her for her effort.

I'd performed an almost-perfect minute-and-a-half routine, and the coach told me I was sloppy. This girl flounced around the room a little, and she got praised. It sure didn't seem fair. It also didn't seem like I had a very good chance at nabbing that last slot on the team.

"Looks like Coach Burrows really wants that girl to be on the squad," I said to Nadia. "I might as well not even try."

"She is coming down hard on you, but that's a good sign."

"A *good* sign?" I asked, sure I hadn't heard her right.

"Yeah. That means she likes you. She treated me rough all last year. How do you think this team got to be number one?"

"I never thought of it that way."

"Come on. You haven't had any tough gymnastic coaches in your life?"

"Not really," I said, thinking about Coach Milligent at Rockdale and Mrs. Turner, my high school coach. Both of them had challenged me, but they'd encouraged me too.

"You've got to make practice more of a priority," Nadia said, "if gymnastics really is important to you."

Gymnastics was important to me. But if I was going to make this team, I was obviously going to have to step outside my comfort zone. Suddenly the world of sororities seemed less significant.

"Thanks, Nadia," I said. We smiled at each other and lined up for the vault.

When I got back to the dorm, Payton was starting to take her laundry to the washroom down the hall, so I decided to join her. After we brought our clean clothes back to the room, we got into a little debate about white sororities versus black ones.

"I heard pledging a black sorority can be really tough," I said.

"Oh yeah," Payton said. "The pledges are hazed badly."

"White sororities haze too," I said, sorting my clothes.

"Not like black ones," she assured me, although she didn't elaborate.

When she asked about my pledging experience, she said she couldn't believe we got to choose from among three.

"If I decided to pledge a sorority," she said, matching her socks, "I couldn't show my face at any other house. If I even thought about pledging somewhere else, the first sorority wouldn't accept me."

"That's crazy," I said. "It doesn't make any sense to me."

"Well, you just don't understand blacks," she said.

"I'm not totally clueless, you know," I said. I reminded her about Robyn, my black girlfriend from high school.

"Oh, and you think that makes you a sista?" Payton asked. "You think you can relate to my world?"

"Hey, what's your problem?" I asked. "I'm not your enemy, you know."

"I know," she said, putting her clothes in the drawers.

"I'm your roommate and your friend . . . and your sister in Christ."

Payton shoved her shirts as tightly into the drawer as she could but still had trouble shutting it. I put down the towel I was folding and went over to help her. Between the two of us, we managed to get the drawer closed.

"I hope you get into the sorority you want," she told me. "I mean, I hope having a black roommate doesn't mess that up for you."

I rolled my eyes, remembering the comment Jewels had

made about that. "You should know better than to listen to Jewels. She always says rude things. Nobody's even asked me who my roommate is."

Payton gave a sigh of relief. It was sweet of her to be so concerned about me. Being in a minority couldn't be easy. I vowed to do everything I could to make her as comfortable as possible.

"Anna is just like Jewels," Payton said, interrupting my thoughts. "She didn't want you to room with me because I'm black. They deserve each other."

"Some people don't realize how hurtful their words are until somebody hurts them. I tried to explain that to Jewels, but I don't know if I got through."

"Well, I'm just going to stay out of it."

That afternoon, I went to the student affairs courtyard to get my final envelope. Jewels was there, and we stood with our arms locked in eager anticipation.

I opened my envelope with trembling fingers, then screamed when I saw my sorority of choice, Alpha Gamma Delta, printed on the card.

Jewels screamed too. Her card was identical to mine. We screamed again and hugged each other tight.

"Where's Anna?" I asked. "I can't wait to tell her the news."

"She got a call earlier today," Jewels said casually. "No sorority chose her, so she was told she didn't need to come for a final envelope."

My heart sank. I prayed God would give Anna peace.

The next evening, all thirty of the new Alpha Gam pledges stood in the basement of the sorority house wearing white robes, vowing to do our best to uphold the fundamental principles and ideals of the sorority dedicated to sisterhood. As we were reciting our vow in unison, I saw a tear fall from Jewels's eye. She was taking her oath seriously.

"I believe in community service," we chanted. "I believe in lifting up my sisters."

I hoped Jewels would be a little more sensitive with Anna now that she was an Alpha Gamma Delta. After all, we were taking a vow not to put other people down just because they weren't part of our elite group.

At the end of the ceremony, Liza, the pledge master, attached the Alpha Gamma Delta pin to my blouse. As she shook my hand and smiled at me, I felt different. Special. I felt included, like I had accomplished something great. I planned to make Liza proud and my grandmother and my mom too.

"I am an Alpha Gamma Delta!" I hollered.

It felt great giving my pledge.

four

fretting
the day

i don't want to get up," I groaned as I stared at my alarm clock on Sunday morning.

The night before had been exhausting with all the new sorority and fraternity members at a big party displaying their pins, colors, and group spirit. Although I saw several guys with KA letters across their shirts, I didn't bump into Branson. I wondered if he was avoiding me. Maybe he'd found a new girlfriend. I shook off the thought and decided to enjoy my evening and make new friends. And that's what I'd done, all night long.

I turned off the alarm and went back to sleep. The next thing I knew, it was 2:15 in the afternoon and I still had no desire to get up. It had been a long time since I'd been able to just sleep a whole day away. I knew I should go to gymnastics practice, but I didn't feel like it. Everybody deserves a day off every now and then, I decided. Besides, I had plenty of time to practice. The last slot on the team wouldn't be decided until the end of the semester.

Payton was gone when I got up. I was glad for the privacy.

When my stomach started rumbling, I crawled out of bed and headed for the refrigerator. I found a green apple and a can of tomato juice. As I sat on my bed munching, I prayed.

Lord, I don't have any energy today. I don't know if I'm dreading my first day of college classes tomorrow or what, but I need strength.

I tossed the empty juice can and the apple core into the plastic-lined wastebasket, then crawled back into bed. Even though I hadn't drunk any alcohol, I still felt like I had a hangover.

At 5:29 I awoke to screaming from the other side of the bathroom. Jewels and Anna were at it again.

What's with those two? I wondered.

I pulled the covers up over my head to drown out the noise, but their racket grew louder until I could hear their words clearly.

"You're going to stretch my shirt," Jewels whined. "How dare you put on my clothes! You're not an Alpha Gamma Delta, and you never will be, so don't pretend."

Anna didn't respond. I figured she was probably crying.

Why does Jewels have to be so mean? I thought.

I felt like I should go over there and try to help Anna, but I didn't know what to say. Maybe it was better if I didn't stick my nose in where it didn't belong. Then again, I thought, things were only going to get worse if somebody didn't do something to stop it.

I threw the sheet off me and dragged myself to the bathroom, where I splashed water on my face. Then I took a deep breath, said a quick prayer for guidance, and opened the adjoining door.

"You guys are being really loud in here," I said. "What's going on?"

Jewels and Anna were standing in front of the closet.

Jewels, hands on her hips, was yelling at Anna, who was wearing Jewels's Alpha Gam sweatshirt. It was way too small for her, and the seams looked like they were about to burst.

Jewels pointed at Anna. "She's trying on my sorority clothes. I caught her looking at herself in the mirror, smiling. As if she could possibly ever be—"

"What's the harm in letting her try on some things?" I asked.

"It's all right," Anna said, barely above a whisper, as she carefully took off the sweatshirt.

Jewels grabbed it out of her hands, then turned toward me with red eyes. "I should have known you'd take her side. Well, if you want to let her stretch out your stuff and go against the rules of our sorority, then you go ahead. But I don't want this blob ruining my clothes." Jewels stormed off into the bathroom.

Anna fell to her bed and started wailing. I sat beside her.

The only thing I could think of to do was pray. I knew she wasn't a Christian, but maybe this was God's way of leading this sweet girl to Him.

I knelt beside her, bowed my head, and placed my hand on her back. "Lord, I pray for Anna right now. I pray that You will help her understand who You are. Things haven't gone quite the way she hoped this first week in college. But I know You can turn bad situations around, and I ask You to do that for her right now. Restore her joy. Take away her disappointment and make her happy. And let her know that I'm here if she needs me. I don't always get all the things I want, either, so I know how it feels. Let her know she can talk to me."

Anna had stopped sobbing. I could tell my words were reaching her.

"Lord, I also pray for Jewels. Please help her to be more sensitive. And I pray for Payton too."

My private moment with Anna was suddenly interrupted when Jewels threw open the bathroom door. "You guys are praying?" she said in a disgusted voice.

I opened my eyes and was about to tell Jewels how rude I thought she was when Anna gave me a huge hug. Jewels mumbled something and headed out into the hall.

Anna and I popped some popcorn, sprinkled some sugar on it, and watched a Disney movie on TV for a few relaxing hours.

Shortly after I returned to my room, the phone rang.

"Laurel," my dad said, and I instantly realized how much I missed his voice.

"Hey, Dad." I wanted to leap through the phone and tell him how much I loved him.

"Everybody at church was asking about you this morning. Told me to say hi to you and let you know they're praying for you."

"Thanks, Dad," I said, my throat so tight I could barely speak.

"You're going to have a wonderful first day of college classes tomorrow," he said.

His words made me feel inspired, excited, and rejuvenated.

Dad put my mother on the phone, and she congratulated me for making it into her old sorority. "Just don't lose focus and start spending too much time on social events," she cautioned me. "Remember, your grades come first."

There was so much I wanted to say to her. I wanted to tell her that I missed her so much I almost wanted to come home. But I didn't want my parents to worry, so I kept my emotions in check.

After she said, "I love you," I got a chance to say a quick hello to my brothers, Liam, Lance, and Luke. I laughed at their stories of the trouble they'd gotten into during the first week of my absence. I missed my family, and I knew they missed me.

After I hung up, I thanked the Lord for my great upbringing and for my family, who loved me. I knew I could face whatever came my way because I didn't have to deal with anything alone. My family was always with me in my heart, and God would always be with me in spirit. I had absolutely nothing to fear.

The next day I got up before dawn so I could get to the gym bright and early. I waltzed in at five o'clock, but I still didn't beat Nadia.

During my high school days, I'd practiced at Rockdale Gym every Monday and Wednesday before school and every Tuesday and Thursday after school, as well as every Saturday morning. When my school started its own gymnastics team during my senior year, we had practices after school every Monday and Wednesday. I'd been known to go into the gym on Sunday evening when a meet was coming up. I wanted to make sure I stayed on top of my game.

But I had taken off the whole last summer, and I was really out of shape.

I watched Nadia doing ab crunches. She was so thin that I felt fat in comparison. If I planned to be a Gym Dawg, I was going to have to get in shape.

Nadia sat up and looked up at me. "It's about time you got here," she teased. "I've been working out for half an hour already."

"That's not fair," I said. "You look like you could run twenty laps around the gym."

"Regular workouts build endurance," Nadia told me. "You should try it." She grinned, and I couldn't help but grin back.

"I do need to be more consistent," I admitted. "But I'm not sure there's anything I can do at this point to make the team. Coach Burrows hardly spends any time with me. I'm sure she doesn't want me on the team."

Nadia walked to the vault. "Just come in to work out more often. Coach Burrows checks the log every day. Right now she probably thinks this is just a hobby to you. She'll start to like you more when you put more effort into trying to make the team."

"I don't know," I said, looking down. "I'm just not sure I have the talent."

"How can you say that?" Nadia lifted my head. "I saw you on the beam the other day. I was blown away by your routine."

"You're kidding. You always score awesome on the beam, and your routines are a lot more difficult than mine."

"I'm nervous every time I get up there. But I can tell from watching you that it's your favorite apparatus. Mix that confidence with coaching from one of the best in the business, and you're going to be awesome."

"I wish Coach Burrows knew that."

"She will," Nadia said with a grin. "When you start showing her what you can do."

When I got back to my dorm room, I only had forty-five minutes to get ready for my first day of classes. I stressed over what to wear, knowing that Georgia in August could be really hot or breezy and cool. After I pulled several outfits out of the closet and tossed them onto the bed, Payton was staring at me like I'd lost my mind.

"What's your problem?" she asked.

I looked at her with huge eyes. "I truly do not know what to wear."

She shrugged her shoulders. "What's the big deal? Just throw on anything."

Payton had on an oversized gray sweat suit. She was obviously comfortable. But the outfit was hardly attractive.

I wondered why Payton was so carefree about her clothes. Her father was wealthy. He made a six-figure income from the car dealership he owned in Augusta. The new car Payton drove was awesome. And yet she dressed like a bum. I envied her, though, because even in her thrown-together outfit she looked adorable.

Well, maybe she could get away with it. But I was an Alpha Gamma Delta and a freshman. I didn't want to make a bad impression on anyone. Jeans and a T-shirt was not the image I wanted to go for.

Payton picked up three outfits from my bed. "This is not a historically black college," she explained. "Now, if I was at Spelman or Howard, I might dress a little nicer. But my classes here are going to be filled with white people. I don't care about impressing any of them."

I wished Brittany were there so I could go through her closet for something to wear. The first day of our senior year, she had practically told me flat out that all my clothes were trash. But she was great about letting me borrow her beautiful outfits. Now my bed was covered in clothes and nothing I had measured up.

I picked up two shirts but decided they weren't the look I was going for. I let out a long sigh.

"OK, you're stressing me out," Payton said, snatching the shirts from my hand. "Just pick something or you're going to be late."

I put on a skirt and blouse, but that looked too dressy. I tried a white pantsuit, but it seemed too country.

"I've got to go," Payton said, shaking her head. "See you later." She gave me a quick hug before dashing out the door.

"I hate this," I grumbled and finally settled on khaki capri pants and a pink cotton blouse. I stood in front of the mirror and stared at the outfit that used to be my favorite.

Although still not completely satisfied, I'd run out of time. Leaving all the clothes on my bed, I picked up my book bag, grabbed my keys, and headed to my first class.

I saw a lot of people asking for directions. But the sorority sisters had given all us pledges a tour around the campus, so I knew where I was going. But all the way to class I wondered what everyone I passed was thinking. Did my outfit look stupid? Was my hair OK?

A group of girls near the library looked my way and started giggling. I was so concerned about whether they were laughing at me, I tripped over an uneven section of sidewalk. All my books went flying and I landed on my tush. The laughter I'd imagined was no longer a fantasy. A small crowd of people gathered around me, and I became the first joke of the new school year.

I grabbed my sorority notebook out of the grass, then reached for my textbooks.

"Alpha Gam sure lowered their standards this year," someone said, apparently noticing my notebook.

Everyone laughed. My cheeks burned and I tried desperately not to cry.

Then I heard an unfamiliar male voice. "If you can't help the lady pick up her things, at least stop gawking and get to class. This isn't elementary school."

I didn't look up, but I heard feet shuffling away.

"Do you need a tissue?" my rescuer asked, picking up my heavy books.

I lifted my eyes and saw a gorgeous man standing above me. He had rusty brown hair and a face that was even more adorable than Branson's or Foster's. I tried not to stare at the strong muscles in his arms and legs.

"Thanks," I said as I took my books from him.

"You know, as heavy as those are, you might want to get a rolling book bag."

I stared at him in a daze. He was so gorgeous, I couldn't even respond to his helpful suggestion. By the time I recovered, he was gone. But his chivalry had put joy back into my day. As I scurried to class, I prayed.

Lord, my day started a little out of whack. Probably because I didn't pray first thing this morning. Forgive me for not putting You first. That little incident reminded me that I can't do this without You. Thanks for sending that guy to help me.

I walked into lit class late. Almost all of the thirty or so chairs were taken. When I stepped into the room, the professor

—a woman about my mom's age, who was wearing a classy skirt suit—stopped talking and nodded at an empty seat in the back.

I sat quickly, then looked up. On the white board at the front of the room was the statement, "Expectations of a freshman at UGA." The words were written in bold red marker.

Professor Bassett spoke to the class in an aggressive tone. "This is how I plan to get to know you all and your writing styles. Don't try to write Shakespearean. Just be yourself. After I assess your papers, I'll know what I need to cover before this term ends."

Mrs. Bassett sat at her desk. Everyone around me started grumbling about having to write a paper on the first day of class. I felt the same way. But getting a good education was the reason I was in college. So I picked up my pencil, welcoming the challenge.

> I have big expectations of being a freshman at the University of Georgia. I want to grow and become more well-rounded academically, athletically, and socially.
>
> I am majoring in Mass Communications with a concentration in journalism. I hope to become a Christian author one day or possibly an anchorwoman for a news station. I don't know what other careers in journalism are possible, but I plan to consider all options.
>
> I am a gymnast and I have always admired the Gym Dawgs team. I want to help them win another national title. Though I am only a walk-on at this point, I believe that being around the best will raise my ability tremendously. It is my dream to participate in the Olympics, but I'll be satisfied if I can compete in the NCAA.
>
> I am not an introvert, but I am not as exciting as I'd like to be. I know I will meet new friends from different walks of life here and that I'll learn from their experiences. I joined a sorority and expect to enjoy it reverently.

I hope to make a big impact on the people I come in contact with. I love the Lord, and before I leave this place I plan to tell all those who don't know Christ who He is.

I also expect love. I have no clue how I'll accomplish this feat, but I want to leave here knowing who I will spend the rest of my life with.

As long as I keep my faith in God, study hard, work out regularly, and have fun, I know I will enjoy my time at the University of Georgia.

I read over my paper a couple of times, corrected the commas, crossed the Ts, and then wrote it all over. I still had an hour to spare.

When I dropped my paper on Professor Bassett's desk, she whispered, "I saw you working. I could tell you wrote from the heart. I'm going to enjoy reading your paper, Miss . . ."

"Shadrach," I said.

"Like in Shadrach, Meshach, and Abednego?" she said, naming the three guys who were thrown into the fiery furnace with Daniel in the Old Testament.

"Yeah." I laughed, thrilled that my professor was familiar with the Bible.

"I'm proud of you, Miss Shadrach. Most of the other students complained about this assignment, but you tackled it head-on and got it done. Keep up this kind of work ethic and you'll do great in my class and probably every other subject you take this semester."

"Thanks," I said, appreciating her compliment.

The rest of my classes went pretty much the same way. I couldn't wait to tell Payton about my day, but when she came into our room, she threw her stuff in a corner and plopped down on the bed.

"How was your day?" I asked.

"Not great," she grumbled. "Nothing catastrophic. But I'm not sure this is the place I should be going to school."

"Really?" I said, sitting beside my friend on her bed. "How come?"

She sniffed. "I miss my family."

I missed my family too. But Payton's dad had come to visit her more often than mine, so I knew there had to be more to her sadness than that.

"I miss my old friends too," she added. "The only guys I ever cared about are here, but I'm no longer with either of them."

I could relate to her feelings, but it was normal for any college freshman to have some trouble adjusting to a new life. I waited for her to get to the heart of the issues she was having.

Payton took a deep breath, obviously trying to hold back tears. "And this place is so . . . white. I really don't feel like I belong."

I couldn't really empathize with her racial struggles, but I sure knew what it was like to feel like I didn't belong somewhere. I took her hand. "I'm sorry today didn't go well. This college stuff is pretty overwhelming for all of us. But that's life. One day we have trails; the next day, triumph." I squeezed her hand. "God is with you every day. I'm sure to-morrow will be better."

"Do you really think so?" she asked, her voice filled with hope.

"I know so," I assured her with a big smile.

She gave me a big hug and thanked me for being such a great friend.

Payton and I had been put together as roommates be-cause we had the same major. She wanted to be a sports an-nouncer and I hoped to cover world news, but we were both in communications. I was excited that we had some of the same courses. Though we didn't take any classes at the same time, we'd be able to study together.

"So," she finally said, getting a soda, "how was your day?"

I chuckled. "It started out kinda miserable because I tripped on the sidewalk and dropped my books."

Payton laughed so hard she almost choked on her drink.

"But then this angel came to my rescue."

With wide eyes, Payton said, "Angel?"

"This really cute guy helped me pick up my books. That changed my whole outlook. His act of kindness gave me a smile all day." Payton grinned at me like she'd just discovered a juicy secret. "It wasn't romantic or anything, just nice, OK?"

"If you say so," Payton said, raising her hands. "So what else happened to you today?"

"My first class was English lit and I wrote a paper about why I'm here."

"You did a paper?" Payton asked. "Guess I'll be doing that tomorrow."

"Professor Bassett is really nice."

"Still," Payton said, her shoulders slumped. "A paper on the first day? You know, college is turning out to be a lot harder than I thought."

"Oh, come on, Payton—smile," I said, doing my best to be encouraging. "We're going to love this place, and we're both gonna do great here. Quit fretting the day."

f i v e

adjusting
to it

t *here's no way I'm gonna make this team,* I told myself as I watched the Gym Dawgs work out. The upperclassmen were performing like professional athletes, effortlessly utilizing techniques I had been struggling with for years.

I knew I was good, but these women were world-class gymnasts. I'd seen them compete on television many times. I was just a small-town girl with a dream. How could I hope to keep up?

"Come on," Nadia said, gesturing for me to join her on the mat where she was doing stretches. "Let's work out together."

"No, no, you go ahead. I'm going to stretch out over there." I pointed to a corner near the bleachers where I didn't think anyone would notice me.

Nadia caught up with me before I was halfway to my corner. "What's going on with you? Are you OK?"

One of the gymnasts, who had just finished an incredible

routine on the parallel bars, scowled at me. "She's scared! Little girl should go back to the community gym. I don't think she's ready to play in the big league."

Nadia defended me. But I just stood there trembling. I couldn't say a thing because I knew the girl was right. I was frightened. At that moment I wanted to walk out of the gym and forget about trying to become a Gym Dawg. It was going to take too much work for me to get even close to good enough. Whatever made me think I could make this team?

"Come on," Nadia said as she pulled me back toward the mat.

I focused straight ahead, trying to avoid making eye contact with anyone, certain that they were all staring at me. I wanted to yell out, "Hey, I don't care what you big, bad people think; I'm gonna make this team." But I couldn't say it because I didn't believe it.

I knew I couldn't just walk away, so I began stretching with Nadia.

The upperclassmen kept whispering taunts behind my back. Finally one girl walked up to me and said, "I hear you're pretty good on the beam. Why don't you show us what you've got?"

Everyone but Nadia snickered.

Suddenly I felt the same way I had back in grade school when I was the last kid to be picked for the softball team.

I walked up to the beam, my stomach doing cartwheels. As soon as I mounted, I fell right off. Everyone snickered. If I could have crawled under the mat and disappeared, I would have. But I was determined not to give up.

I jumped back up on the beam, but within seconds, I fell again. The taunts increased in volume and intensity. Assistant Coach Ide told everyone to be quiet and encouraged me to try once more. I did. But halfway through the routine, I fell a third time.

I hunched my shoulders against the barrage of angry, discouraging words and crept to the back of the group.

Summer Love, the cute African-American girl, brushed by me and stepped onto the mat. Seizing the opportunity I'd left open to her, she started showing off her skills.

She moved across the floor with precision and grace. I didn't know if rhythm came easily to her because she was black or because she was a naturally good dancer or because she had worked hard and taken lessons for years. But whatever the reason, she looked awesome.

"Wow," I heard several people whisper as they watched her beautiful dance routine.

When Summer finished, Nadia performed an outstanding uneven bar routine. As I watched, my heart was thrilled to see such a magnificent performance. But at the same time my spirit was sinking as I watched my chances of making the team dwindle into nothingness.

Just then a voice whispered in my ear, "Nice going, Shadrach." I turned and saw Summer standing close beside me. "I was nervous about getting that last spot, but after watching your pitiful performance, I know I'll get in. You might as well give up now."

I felt my pulse start racing. I had no intention of just giving up!

I headed straight for the balance beam. I'd show everyone in this room, including that instigator Summer Love, exactly what I could do.

As soon as I reached the beam, Coach Burrows caught my eye and nodded in the direction of her office.

I followed her in. As soon as the door was closed, I asked, "Did I do something wrong?"

"No," she said. "I just needed to speak with you." She sat behind her desk and motioned for me to take a seat too, which I did. "I don't like what I'm seeing from you, Laurel."

"I'm pretty disappointed with my performance too," I admitted, focusing on the carpet.

"You can't let outside distractions deter you from staying focused. You have to find a way to maintain your composure."

I looked up at her. She looked genuinely concerned for me.

Coach Burrows stood, walked toward me, and leaned against the corner of her desk. "You're a dynamic young lady with a lot of talent. Tune the upperclassmen out. You're a freshman; they're just trying to make it tough on you. You've got to learn how to ignore them."

But, I wanted to say, *if I ignore everybody, they'll never accept me.* I wanted so much to fit in with the team. That was one of the main reasons I came to the University of Georgia.

"Now," she continued, crossing her arms, "I've heard you have a few extracurricular activities going on."

"Only one," I corrected her. "I joined a sorority."

"That's fine. But most top gymnasts find they don't have time for anything other than classes and practice." She handed me a sheet of white paper. I gave her a puzzled expression, then looked at the sheet. On it was a typed roster of the gymnastics team. At the bottom was one blank spot. "I'd honestly like to see your name on that last line, Laurel."

"I want that too," I said.

She walked behind her desk again. "Then don't overload yourself with other activities. If you want that last slot, you've got to earn it."

"I promise," I said with determination, "my sorority activities will not interfere with my gymnastics performance."

She looked at me for a long moment, weighing my words. "All right, then," she said, giving me a quick nod and a slight smile. "Get back to practicing."

"Come on, Jewels," I said as my suite mate stood in the bathroom wiping green gunk off her face. "We're going to be late." I'd promised Jewels we could go to the first pledge class meeting together, but she was taking forever to get ready.

"It's almost six o'clock," I told her, hoping that would

hurry her up. She still had curlers in her hair and was wearing a robe and bunny slippers.

I didn't want to go to the meeting alone, but I didn't want to be late either. "I'm just going to walk," I said.

"Fine," Jewels replied, blotting her face with a towel. "If you can't wait a few more minutes, then go. I have a feeling I'm going to be nominated for pledge class president, so I want to look my cutest."

"I'll see you at the sorority house," I said, grabbing my purse. "Even with you driving and me walking, I'm sure I'll beat you there."

"What route are you taking?" she asked as she squirted toothpaste on her toothbrush. "If I see you along the way, I'll stop and pick you up."

"Don't worry about it," I said, looking at my watch again. "The meeting starts in twenty minutes. It'll only take me ten to walk there. You won't even be out of the house for another half hour." I picked up my pledge book and hurried out the door.

When I neared the sorority house, I noticed that all the other new pledges wore clothes in our sorority colors, burgundy and green, just like I did. There were thirty girls in our group, and I was eager to get to know everyone.

As I started up the stairs to the house, two girls I remembered seeing at the pledge activities came up to me.

"Hi," the shorter one said with a bright grin. "My name is Jill. I'm from South Carolina."

"My name's Mandelyn," the taller girl said, her slight smile revealing the glint of braces. "I'm from Alabama."

"We're roommates," Jill told me. "Same dorm as you, one floor above."

"That's great!" I exclaimed, excited to meet two new friends.

The three of us signed in at the door and then entered the living room, where several other pledges were already mingling.

When I told Jill and Mandelyn that I was a gymnast, they acted really excited and asked all kinds of questions. As I talked about my sport, more girls listened in. I started feeling self-conscious about being the center of attention, but everyone seemed genuinely interested in me, and it felt great.

Finally deciding to let someone else talk, I asked if anyone else in the group was trying out for a sport. A few of the girls started talking about women's basketball. I listened for a while, then decided to go get some punch.

As I passed the foyer, I overheard Liza, the pledge director, tell Julie Anne that only twenty-nine pledges had signed in. A knot formed in my stomach. I knew which girl was late.

"I can't believe my sister would do this," Julie Anne seethed under her breath. Then she turned and addressed the group in a stern voice. "Pledges, it's time to call this meeting to order, but one of your class members is late. Because of that you all have to come here on Saturday morning and clean the sorority house."

"Why do we all have to suffer for the actions of one person?" Jill whined.

The room fell silent, except for a couple of gasps. I couldn't believe Jill had questioned Julie Anne.

"If one pledge gets in trouble," Julie Anne replied, "all of you will *suffer*." Julie Anne stormed down the stairs. Liza told the rest of us to follow so we could get started on the program.

When we were all settled into chairs, Liza asked us to stand one at a time and tell a little about ourselves. "No more than one minute per person, please, or we'll be here all day."

Everyone chuckled, appreciating the humor that lightened the mood Julie Anne had created in response to Jewels's tardiness.

When my turn came, I stood and said, "I'm Laurel

Shadrach from Conyers, Georgia. As most of you know now, I'm a gymnast. I'm also the daughter of a pastor, and I have three younger brothers who are all a year apart. I've always tried to be a good girl, but I'm not perfect. I've had my share of struggles, but they've made me stronger and brought me closer to God." I felt good inside about declaring my faith boldly in front of these girls.

"My mother was an Alpha Gamma Delta at the University of Arkansas," I added, "and so was her mom. Being part of a sorority really means a lot to me. Especially this one. I think Alpha Gam is the best sorority on any campus, and I'm proud to be a member."

The girls all stood and cheered, like they had for everyone else who'd introduced themselves. As I took my seat again and the next girl started speaking, I noticed Jewels standing in the back of the room, glaring at me. I also saw Julie Anne glaring at her. I shook my head and focused on the girl who was talking.

After all the girls who were seated had introduced themselves, Liza said it was time to announce the nominations for pledge class president. Jewels quietly took a seat in the back.

"This year, for the first time ever, the upperclassmen of Alpha Gamma Delta have come up with only one nomination for the position of pledge class president."

I glanced at Jewels. She was sitting up straight on the edge of her chair, a confident smile plastered across her face. She looked like a magazine model—her hair perfectly curled, her cheeks glowing with soft pink blusher, her proud lips outlined in a stunning shade that almost matched her red hair. This was her moment of glory, and she was going to relish every second of it.

I really did want Jewels to be nominated because I knew how much she wanted it. But I also kinda wished someone else would be our pledge class president just because of Jewels's snooty attitude.

All the girls were whispering among themselves, speculating on whom the one nominee might be. Apparently not everyone knew about Jewels being Julie Anne's sister.

"The sole nomination for this year's pledge class president," Liza said dramatically, "is Laurel Shadrach."

My heart sank. I didn't want to be president. I already had too many responsibilities. The promise I'd made to Coach Burrows about not letting my sorority activities interfere with gymnastics rang in my ears.

But all the girls in the room—except Jewels, who had disappeared—were giving me a standing ovation. Liza was smiling broadly at me, applauding wildly. Julie Anne encouraged me to come forward. When I did, the noise in the room grew louder for a few moments. I waited for the girls to quiet down, then cleared my throat.

"I don't know what to say," I stammered. Everyone chuckled. "This is such a huge honor. I'm already committed to so many things here; if anyone else had been nominated, I would have backed out of the race." The room grew quiet. Liza and Julie Anne looked at me with quizzical expressions. "But I don't want to let my pledge class down. Since I was the only one nominated," I said, "I accept the challenge."

The place burst into excited applause again. I felt myself blushing.

"How about a speech?" Liza suggested.

I stared at her. I hadn't been prepared for this. I looked at Julie Anne.

"Go on," she said. "Just say what's on your mind and heart."

Without thinking much about it, I blurted, "Can the pledge class president challenge the decision to make everyone come in on Saturday morning and clean the sorority house?"

I gulped. I couldn't believe I'd said something so impulsive. But then I thought, *What have I got to lose? The worst thing they can probably do is change their minds about making me pledge class president!*

Julie Anne stared at me for a moment, obviously aghast that I had questioned her decision. But Liza started laughing. And then the rest of the girls joined in. Pretty soon even Julie Anne's stern face cracked. "All right," she said, rolling her eyes. "I guess the whole group doesn't have to pay for one person's mistake."

Every girl in the room rushed up to me, surrounding me with love and appreciation and congratulations. I looked around for Jewels. She was nowhere in sight.

I thanked everyone for their support, telling them that I would need their help to do my job well. They all assured me that they would assist in any way they could.

When people started spreading out into small groups, getting involved in their own conversations, I rushed to the bathroom. When I burst through the door, I saw Jewels standing at the sink, her perfect makeup smeared, her hair and clothes disheveled.

"I'm sorry," I said quietly.

She glared at me, and I expected a torrent of heated words to spew forth. But her pursed lips stayed tightly closed and her face grew red with stifled wrath. After her seething eyes bore a hole through my soul, she turned around and stormed out of the room. The banging of the bathroom door against the wall echoed down the hall.

After taking care of business in the bathroom, I looked around for Julie Anne. When I found her I told her I hoped I hadn't embarrassed her in front of the pledges by questioning her authority.

"Just don't do it again," she said with a grin.

I lowered my voice. "I didn't figure you'd want everyone to hate your sister for getting them into trouble."

She looked at me with sorrow in her eyes, but after a brief moment, the sadness disappeared and she smiled at me again. "You know," she said with a chuckle, "you're go-ing to make a great class president."

———————

"What's her problem?" Payton asked when Jewels woke us up early the next morning by slamming the bathroom door between our rooms.

"She's mad at me," I explained, crawling out of bed.

"What did you do to her?"

I didn't want to brag, but Jewels had been a brat to both of us. I felt both good and bad about defeating her. "I'm the pledge class president."

"You go, girl!" We slapped hands.

"She really wanted this, and I didn't. But now that I have it, I'm really excited. All the girls respect me. It's great. But I still feel bad for Jewels."

"She doesn't deserve your sympathy," Payton said, checking the outfits in her closet. "It's about time she felt what other people feel."

What Payton said made sense, but I still felt guilty for getting something Jewels wanted so much. I didn't know what I could do to make her feel better, though, so I decid-ed to just stay out of her way.

"So, what does it mean to be a pledge class president?" Payton asked, pulling a pair of jeans off a hanger. "What do you have to do?"

I shrugged. "I don't really know everything yet. But this afternoon we're going to the KA fraternity house to watch the football game on their big-screen TV."

"That sounds like fun," Payton said.

"Yeah, I guess." I sat down on my bed, still in my paja-mas.

"You don't sound very excited. Don't you want to go?"

"Not really," I admitted. "Branson's in that fraternity."

Payton slipped into her denims. "Oh, girl, don't worry about him."

"I've got an idea!" I exclaimed, springing from my bed. "Why don't you come to the party with me?"

She raised her eyebrows. "Me? Go to an all-white frat house? Uh-uh!"

"It won't be all day. The game starts at one, so it should be over around four."

"That's still too long for me."

I clasped my hands together, practically begging her to come. "They're having a barbecue."

"Really? What kind of food?"

"Hamburgers, chicken, and ribs."

"Hmm," Payton said, slowly pulling a T-shirt over her hair.

"And I've heard the KAs are excellent chefs."

She popped her head through the neck of the shirt and emerged with a big smile. "In that case, I'm in!"

"Thanks," I said, hugging her.

That afternoon, when we walked into the KA house, everyone stared at us and started whispering to one another. Suddenly I felt bad about inviting Payton. She was the only black person in the place.

Payton leaned over and said, "Maybe I shouldn't have come."

"Don't say that," I said. "My friends are cool."

"I hope so."

Jill and Mandelyn called me over to their corner of the room. "Come on," I said to Payton. She followed me. I wondered if my new friends were going to lecture me on bringing a black girl into our circle. They didn't say more than "hi" to Payton, but they didn't reprimand me for my choice of company or do anything mean to her.

More people came up and started talking to me, and I soon lost track of Payton. Then all of a sudden I heard her scream. I went in search for her and found her in the game room, staring at the TV, jumping up and down.

"Go, Dakari! That's my man! Awesome!"

Dakari Graham was the halfback of our football team. I'd met him my first day at college. He put a fist through our window when he caught Payton's ex-boyfriend Tad at the dorm.

Jill asked me if my friend knew Dakari "The Bomb" Graham. When I explained that he was her ex-boyfriend, she squealed, "Really?"

"That's awesome," Mandelyn added. Both of them went over to the couch and started talking to Payton. I shook my head and smiled.

As I stood there watching Payton make friends with my new friends, I noticed Branson in the crowd surrounding her. He looked so handsome. His skin was nicely tanned, and his blond hair had a few black streaks in it. My heart melted.

"Would you like a beer?" he asked Payton in his smooth, sexy way.

"I don't drink," she said, her focus riveted on the TV. "How about a cola?"

"Sure." He took off toward the kitchen.

When he was out of sight, I worked my way through the crowd to Payton's side. "That guy who just offered you a drink is Branson Price," I whispered in her ear.

"Really?" she said. "He's cute."

"Yeah, I know." I sighed. "Do you think you could put in a few good words for me? At least find out where we stand?"

"I don't want to get into the middle of your business," she said. "I wouldn't know what to say."

"Come on, Payton. Please?" I begged. "I love him."

She sighed. "All right."

I thanked her, then sauntered over to the bar where Mandelyn and Jill were getting drinks.

"Laurel, we are so glad you're our pledge class president," Mandelyn said, sipping her soda.

"Yeah," Jill added. "You've really got what it takes to be a good one."

I heard their accolades but wasn't really concentrating on what they were saying. I was watching Branson and Payton talking, hoping she could convince him that I needed to be in his life.

"I couldn't believe it when you questioned Julie Anne's authority right off," Jill said, giggling. "But I sure am glad you got us out of cleaning the house on Saturday."

"Me too," Mandelyn said. "You're the best!"

"Thanks," I mumbled.

Just then, Julie Anne yelled out, "Hey, Laurel!" I looked across the room and saw Jewels's sister sitting on a chair with a turned-over plate of nachos on her lap. "Can you bring me a couple of napkins?"

I grabbed a few off the bar, then hurried to Julie Anne's rescue. As she mopped up the mess, I glanced at Branson and Payton. Their conversation didn't seem to be going too well, but he was smiling. For a moment I thought he was smiling at me, but then I realized his eyes were focused on Jill and Mandelyn.

And they were smiling back!

Please, God, don't let this happen again! Don't let my friends come between me and Branson. Lord, please help Payton talk him into believing in us again.

I knew I could no longer settle for the way things had been, with us being apart. I just wasn't adjusting to it.

needing
His direction

Why did he storm away like that? I asked myself as Branson left Payton's side.

She looked concerned, like she wanted to continue their conversation. When he didn't come back, she relaxed on the couch and continued watching the football game on TV.

I crossed the room and plopped down beside her. "OK, tell me everything," I whispered. "What did he say? Will he take me back? Does he want me? Can we work it out?"

"He's gonna think about it," she said without taking her eyes off the television. When the play ended, she turned to me. "Look at yourself. You're all worked up over this guy. Just enjoy the party. Go have some fun."

I knew her advice made sense. But how could I relax? I wanted to grab Payton's arm and force her to help me get Branson back.

Frustrated, I went back to the bar and did something I

knew I'd probably regret later, but at the moment I didn't care. "Can I have a wine cooler, please?"

I downed the drink quickly, then ordered another. After the second one, I had an enormous headache, and my heartache didn't feel a bit better.

When I stood up, my head felt foggy and my legs wobbled. I tried to walk over to Payton to tell her I wanted to leave, but before I could take two steps, I fell flat on my face on the floor. The loud thump attracted everyone's attention, and when I looked up, I saw Branson staring at me, shaking his head sadly.

I tried to get up, but my wobbly knees had rug burns and really hurt. I looked around for Jill or Mandelyn or somebody to help me. But everyone had abandoned me, leaving me alone on the floor. I started to cry.

The tears flowed and flowed, and I couldn't stop them. My weeping grew louder. People were glancing at me like I was a disgusting loser, but I couldn't help myself.

Suddenly a group of people came out of the game room, all chatting about the final score. When Payton saw me sitting on the floor wailing, she stopped in midstride, a shocked look on her face. Just before she reached me, my stomach churned violently and I threw up all over her shoes.

Everyone in the room, including the group who'd just finished watching the football game, groaned in disgust and scrambled outside for some fresh air. Payton stepped around the mess I'd made, reached under my armpits, and lifted me up, half carrying me to the bathroom.

After she got the two of us cleaned up, she led me out a back door. The fresh air sobered me up a little as we headed toward the dorm together. But I still had trouble keeping my balance. As Payton badgered me about drinking, I watched the sidewalk carefully, trying to walk in a straight line.

Though my head was still pounding, I started to feel silly. For some reason I couldn't stay on the sidewalk. My feet simply wouldn't go where I wanted them to. I started to giggle. I laughed harder, twirling and weaving and dancing to the music in my head.

An uneven spot in the concrete tripped me up and I tried to catch my balance, but the curb got in my way. I felt Payton grab my arm and yank me hard.

"What'd you do that for?" I asked, staring at her.

"You almost got run over by a car, you idiot!" she yelled.

"I did?" I said stupidly, staring at the road.

"If I hadn't been here, you'd be a bloody mess on the street right now," she said sternly. "You wanna die? Or go into a coma? Or be paralyzed for the rest of your life just because you thought alcohol would make your heartache go away?"

Being reminded of Branson, combined with the realization that I'd almost thrown away my whole life, brought me down from my giddiness fast. "You don't have to lecture me," I grumbled. "I feel bad enough already."

"I hope you do!"

"Look," I said, "I'll be OK. I just have to get back to the dorm and sleep it off."

"That's not all you have to do," Payton said, continuing her lecture. "You need to learn how to deal with disappointment. You've got to turn things over to God. Trust me, Laurel, no guy is worth drowning yourself in booze over."

When we finally reached the dorm room, I took a long, hot shower. When I got out of the bathroom, Payton was gone, but there were two aspirin and a cup of water on my nightstand. I smiled at my friend's thoughtfulness and took the pills.

On my bed I found a note from Payton telling me her dad had come to take her home for the Labor Day weekend. "Get some rest," she advised.

As I crawled into bed, I thanked God for giving me a friend who cared so much about me.

I stayed in my room for most of the three-day weekend,

only going out to stock up the refrigerator. I didn't want to see anybody or talk to anyone. I just wanted to sleep. And relax. And pray. Mostly pray.

But my prayers felt empty. I missed Branson. I wanted him. I needed him. My life was incomplete without him. I couldn't wait for Payton to get back from her parents' house so she could tell me what he said about us getting back together.

On Monday evening, as I was taking yet another nap, the jiggle of the doorknob startled me. When the door opened, I saw Payton standing there with her bags in her hand.

"Welcome back," I said, jumping up to help her with her bags.

"Thanks," she said, accepting my assistance.

I sat on my bed, scratching my unwashed hair, watching her unpack.

"You feeling better?" Payton asked. "Or are you still stressing out about Branson?"

I went to the refrigerator and got out a can of soda for her. "I slept a lot and prayed a lot. So yeah, I do feel better. But . . ." I handed her the drink.

"You're still dying to know what he said to me at the party, right?"

"Yeah," I admitted.

She took several gulps. "All right." She sat on her bed and took another long drink.

I stared at her. "Well? Do I have a chance with him or not?"

She sighed. "Look, I'm sorry, but he said you two want different things, and he doesn't want to compromise."

I collapsed onto my bed.

"Laurel," Payton said, coming over and sitting beside me, "you've got to get over that jerk."

"No," I said, looking up at her with teary eyes. "We're meant to be together. Don't you understand? I just need to find out what he wants and . . . give it to him."

"Don't go there," she warned.

"I'll do whatever it takes to keep Branson." I stood, ready to go find him that minute.

Payton pulled me back down. "What do you think that would prove? You'll just add more misery to the situation. You know God wouldn't be pleased."

I sat down on the bed again, disgusted by what I had just been thinking. "I know you're right. How could I even consider compromising my beliefs over Branson Price?"

My stomach started to hurt like I had cramps. I got off the bed, fell to my knees, and sobbed.

"Lord," I heard Payton whisper, "You've got to help Laurel, 'cause I don't know what to say."

Her words echoed in my heart. *Lord, You've got to help me. I don't know what to do.* I couldn't pray. I couldn't get off my knees. I couldn't even catch my breath.

I knew I loved Branson with all my heart or I wouldn't be in so much pain about losing him. Part of me would be lost forever if Branson and I went our separate ways for good. Maybe that would be for the better. But at the moment it hurt. I felt like I was dying.

Branson and I had talked about getting married all through high school. We'd discussed our wedding plans. The children we were going to have. Our house, our cars, our wonderful life together. Now it had all vanished.

Payton laid her hand on my shoulder. "Lord, Laurel and I are both hurting over boyfriend issues. Please show us what to do. We're coming to You with broken hearts that need mending. Guide us and give us direction. Help us to relax and know that You are in control. We love You and we praise You. Amen."

As she prayed, relief filled my heart. When I got off my knees, I felt renewed hope. I gave Payton a long, tight hug and thanked her for her prayer and her friendship. Then I went to my dresser and picked out some clothes to wear.

"Hey, something just came to me," Payton said. "On my

way into town today, I saw a church that was having a revival. I don't know anything about that place, but as I was praying just now, it occurred to me that maybe you and I should check it out. What do you think?"

"Sounds great," I said. "Let's go tonight."

That night, Payton led me to the little chapel she'd seen. It was called Bald Rock Baptist Church. On the sign behind the pulpit, the B in *Bald* and the c in *Rock* were missing. That distracted me a little but not as much as the fact that I was the only white person in the whole congregation.

I hated to admit it, but I felt uncomfortable. The worship was too charismatic for my taste. Folks were screaming, fainting, sweating, running up and down the aisles, and speaking in tongues. I slouched in my seat at the end of the pew and tried to blend in.

I looked at Payton and saw a frown of skepticism on her face too.

A large balding man came running down the aisle, all out of breath, and fell to the ground right next to my purse. I wondered if he was trying to get into it. I hated thinking that way, but I didn't know these people.

When the man picked himself up and headed farther down the aisle, I picked up my purse and clutched it tightly. I didn't have much money, but what I did have I wanted to keep.

The choir sang "Give Me a Clean Heart." I'd heard the song before but never that way. They were singing with a beat and swaying to the music. It was actually pretty awesome. The words spoke to my soul, and I remembered I was in church to be renewed and revived, not to judge and condemn. I needed to be inspired and uplifted.

The song mentioned staying focused on God. That's what I needed to do. I wanted my heart to be focused on

God. I wanted it to be clean and strong. I wanted to be revived so I could serve God with a pure heart.

Two ladies in the front jumped up and started clapping their hands as they swayed back and forth. My spirit wouldn't let me sit any longer. I stood up and started moving to the beat. The rhythm flowed through my soul. I was excited. This wasn't about me. It was about God answering my prayers by giving me what I needed, not just what I thought I wanted. I needed Him to grant me internal things, like peace, faith, and love. And a clean heart. So that's what I asked Him for.

The tension between Payton and me vanished. When the song ended, we smiled at each other.

A pastor in a blue robe got up from his chair on the podium and approached the pulpit. He spoke passionately about Philippians 4:13, "I can do all things through Christ which strengtheneth me." As he spoke, I knew God was speaking to me. He was telling me I could do nothing on my own, but through Christ all things were possible. "All things," the pastor explained, included whatever God wanted for me. I claimed that promise as my own.

I left the church that night with hope in my heart. Unfortunately that hope lasted for about a week. By the time Sunday came around again, I was feeling deflated and depressed. I wanted to go to church again, but I wasn't sure the Baptist church was the best place for me to attend on a regular basis.

I didn't know how to find the right church, so I called my dad. He recommended a nondenominational one near the campus. On Sunday morning, I dragged Payton there.

I was sure she felt just as uncomfortable in the all-white congregation as I had at the black church. But this worship service was more like what I was used to. The building was new looking and the congregation was much more laid-back. The parishioners looked refined in their dressy clothes, but they weren't too uptight to rejoice. The lyrics to the hymns were projected onto a big screen, and when the people sang, there was no swaying or shouting, just lifting voices to God in praise.

When the choir started singing "There's a Sweet, Sweet Spirit," Payton loosened up a little and started singing along.

I was wondering if this would be my new home church even before the pastor approached the pulpit. I felt connected to God and refreshed. I knew my heavenly Father was in that sanctuary.

When the pastor gave us the Word, I felt even more at home. He spoke from Isaiah 40:31. "They that wait upon the Lord shall renew their strength," he quoted. "They shall mount up with wings as eagles; they shall run, and not be weary; and they shall walk, and not faint."

He talked about waiting times, when you've asked God for something and you have to wait for Him to give it to you.

I'd asked God for Branson. Deep in my heart I wanted God to fix our relationship. I wanted Him to change Branson's heart so he would stand with me for Christ. But if that's not what He wanted, I needed God to give me the strength to be happy with His will for my life.

"Turn with me to Psalm 13," the pastor said.

Payton and I opened our Bibles and started flipping the pages.

"Let's look closely at this passage. David was frustrated with waiting for something in his life. In the first two verses, he asked the Lord why God hadn't changed his situation." The pastor seemed to look directly at me. "Are you waiting for God to do something? Are you angry that what you want hasn't happened yet? It's OK to be angry with God. David was. The Lord knows what you're thinking. He wants you to talk to Him about it. Don't respond to your anger by drinking or getting depressed or shouting at your family. Instead, just tell God how you feel."

I felt like God was talking straight to me. I had been so depressed about Branson that I'd actually resorted to drinking a couple of wine coolers. I knew God could change Branson's heart like He'd changed David's. I was angry about things not working out the way I wanted them to. I was glad to hear this pastor say that it was OK for me to feel that way.

"But David didn't stop there," the pastor continued. "In verses 3 and 4, he asked God to reveal to him what he was doing to block the blessing he wanted." Again, the pastor seemed to look right into my eyes. "Are you blocking your blessing? If you are not reading the Bible faithfully, fasting, and praying, you are not doing what is necessary for God to move in your life."

I'd been doing some ungodly things the last few days. Instead of trying to convince Branson to take me back, and then turning to alcohol when that didn't work, I should have fasted, claimed Scripture, and trusted Him with everything. I needed to work on my relationship with Christ. How could I be a great girlfriend, for Branson or anybody else, if my heart wasn't right with God?

"Verses 5 through 6," the pastor went on, "say that while David waited, he praised God, even though he didn't have what he wanted. Isaiah 40:31 tells us that those who wait upon the Lord will fly with the eagles. They won't get weary when they run. Praise God! He is awesome and He loves you. Even if He doesn't do another thing for you ever, you've got enough to praise Him for. Decide today to be renewed, to wait God's way."

As I sat in that pew, I decided to accept the pastor's challenge. I knew God would help me deal with waiting. I was through with being sad. I was going to praise God for *everything*.

"I can't believe that tramp!" Payton screamed as she came into our room and slammed the door.

"What's the matter?" I asked, taking a break from polishing my nails at the desk Payton and I shared.

She started pacing around the small room, mumbling angry words under her breath.

Putting down the bottle of clear fingernail polish, I stood in front of Payton, blocking her path. "Either calm down or tell me why you're so upset."

Red eyes, burning with hatred, bore into mine. "You want to know why I'm angry? I'll tell you in one word: *Jewels.*"

"What did she do this time?" I asked.

"She came on to Dakari!"

"Your ex-boyfriend?" I asked in shock.

"I was out there in the hallway talking to him, and that . . . that *chick* cut in and practically threw herself at him." Payton started pacing again. "And she's not the only one acting like a fool over my man. You know, ever since Dakari started making a name for himself out there on the football field, all these white girls have started throwing their long, stringy hair all over his fine black body. I'm sick of it!"

I didn't necessarily agree with her on the race thing, but Jewels knew Dakari was involved with Payton. I had no idea why she would get in the middle of that. Then again, Jewels didn't care about anyone except herself. And Dakari was really popular. Jewels probably wanted the kind of attention he was getting. I knew she couldn't really like Dakari. She'd been very clear, on the first day I met her, that she didn't want to even share a room with a black girl. Surely she wouldn't date a black guy.

Payton bent over the dresser, grasping the edges so tightly her knuckles were white. I had no idea what to say to her. How could I help her calm down when I was angry too?

I placed my hand on Payton's shoulder. "Don't worry about Jewels. Dakari probably doesn't even know she exists."

She turned around and looked at me, her eyes brimming with tears. "He was flirting back with her."

I took a tissue from the box on the dresser and handed it to her. "I'm sure he was only doing that to get to you."

"Do you think so?" she said, blotting her eyes.

"This is your chance to let Dakari know that you don't want him to be with anybody but you. If he's going out of his way to get you riled up, that's a clear sign that he cares."

"I don't think so." Payton threw the tissue into the wastebasket forcefully. "They made a date."

I stifled a gasp. How could even Jewels be so insensitive?

"Look," I said, "you need to get your mind off this. Let's go out tonight. Just you and me."

"No," she grumbled. "I've got a lot of studying to do. Besides, I wouldn't be very good company."

"I've got work to do too. How about we go to the library? Then we can grab a bite to eat afterward."

"I don't know," she said, although I could tell she was tempted by my offer.

"Come on. You've been there for me. Now let me be there for you."

She gave me a small grin, then shrugged her shoulders. "All right," she agreed.

After an hour or so of studying at the library, Payton and I went out for dinner and then to a movie. We chose a sappy chick flick, hoping it would make us both feel better.

When we got back to the dorm, I considered having a talk with Jewels to see if she really planned on going through with the date she'd made with Dakari. But she was still so mad at me over the pledge class president nomination, I didn't figure she'd give me a straight answer. My interference might even push her into taking things a step further.

Besides, Dakari was a jerk to make a date with Payton's suite mate in the first place. I wanted to throw him, and Branson, into quicksand.

While Payton was in the bathroom taking a shower, I lay on my bed, crying. Branson hadn't been answering my calls. He'd made it clear to Payton that he didn't want to see me.

He was going on without me, but it seemed that my life could not go on without him. *I'm sick of this,* I thought as I punched the mattress. *Why can't I get over him?*

Payton came out of the bathroom wearing jeans and a nice blouse, her hair and makeup all done up like she was going out. When she saw me crying, she said, "You still whining about that boy? Look, girl, you've got to get over it and move on. That's what I'm gonna do." She tossed her dirty clothes into the hamper.

"But I can't stop loving Branson," I wailed.

"Girl, you ain't trying hard enough."

"I'm not as tough as you are," I said.

"Well, you'd better get tough," she said, grabbing her purse, "or you're gonna spend your whole life crying into your pillow." She strutted out of the room, whistling.

I stared at the door, wondering if Payton was really over Dakari or just putting on a brave front. Then I wiped my cheeks and tried to compose myself like Payton obviously had. *Maybe I should take a shower too,* I thought. It had seemed to work wonders for my roommate's outlook.

I forced myself off the bed and started looking for a towel when I heard a tentative knock at the door. Before I could answer it, the door opened slowly and Julie Anne peeked inside.

"Mind if I come in?" she asked.

I really didn't want to get into sorority stuff at that moment, but I didn't want to offend the Alpha Gamma Delta president, so I nodded. She came in and closed the door softly.

"I ran into your roommate in the hall," she said. "She told me you were down about a guy." She sat on my messed-up bed. "Want to talk about it?"

Julie Anne was the last person I wanted to air my dirty laundry to. I wanted to impress this girl by showing her my strengths, not let her see my vulnerabilities and weaknesses. Besides, she was Jewels's sister. How could I be sure she wouldn't go blab about my pain to a suite mate who was mad at me and might somehow use that knowledge against me?

Julie Anne reached up and touched my arm. "You need to let this out to someone. I promise, anything you share with me will stay between us. As sorority president I have private and personal discussions with girls a lot, and I understand the importance of confidentiality."

I hesitated, still not sure if I could trust her but really wanting to talk to someone who wouldn't tell me to "just get over it" like Payton had.

Julie Anne patted the space next to her on the bed. "I hate to see such a strong, vibrant girl like you feeling down. If I can help, I really want to."

I sat on the bed and started opening up. I ended up talking nonstop for about a half hour. When I finished complaining about my life, Julie Anne told me about all the great things I had going for myself and how I didn't need to feel like a broken romantic relationship was the end of the world.

I had to admit, her pep talk did make me feel a lot better. I thanked her for listening and for offering me compassion.

"No problem," she said, standing. "Any time you need to talk, I'm here for you."

After she left I got on my knees beside the bed. "Lord, thank You for sending Julie Anne to me," I prayed aloud. "I'm tired of struggling. I want to have joy. I want my heart to be free. Please help me. I'm turning all this anxiety over to You. I love You so much, God. No one loves me unconditionally the way You do. I'm ready to start trusting in that love. In Jesus' name, amen."

When I got up I felt revived. After pulling a soda out of the refrigerator, I opened my Bible. I knew what I needed to do to keep myself from being depressed, to stay happy and upbeat. The key was taking the time to worship. I was desperately needing His direction.

s e v e n

thinking
I can

time flew by at school. Between classes, practices, pledge meetings, and studying, it was October before I knew it. The leaves changed, displaying gorgeous fall colors.

My job of pledge class president was going well. I ran meetings tight, always starting and ending on time. I made sure all the ladies in my class knew their sorority history. The upperclassmen gave three different tests over a two-week period, and we all passed each one on the first round.

Liza told me I was the best pledge class president in the sorority's history. She even said so in front of the entire class. The girls responded with more glowing compliments. Even the big sisters said nice things to me about what a great job I was doing.

I basked in all the attention, but I could tell it burned Jewels badly. She stopped speaking to me. I hated that she was jealous, but what could I do?

I was getting adjusted to my classes, which were sort of

hard at first. When I tightened up on my studying, I was able to do a lot better.

Time was even healing my Branson wound. He wasn't gone from my heart, but it didn't hurt as badly anymore.

Gymnastics was the one battle I couldn't seem to conquer. I was going into the gym every morning for early practice, and when no one else was around, I performed difficult routines with confidence, not missing a single move. But when the coach and the other gymnasts were there, I couldn't seem to do anything well.

So what if everybody's watching? I told myself as I stood on the balance beam, one foot in front of the other, my arms extended to keep my balance. *I can do this.*

"Come on, freshman," I heard somebody yell out.

"Are you going to do something or just stand there?" another girl said.

"We're ready when you are, Laurel," the coach said.

I wasn't ready but I had to do something. I finally attempted the first trick in my routine, a front tuck mount. I fell off the beam. The room echoed with laughter.

Not wanting to repeat my triple fall from before, I simply stepped aside and let Summer perform. *I might as well just give the last spot on the team to her.*

Over the last few weeks, Summer Love had become a dynamic gymnast. She showed great confidence on the mat and had picked up impressive skills on the uneven bars. Her natural grace made the tricks she did look simple and almost perfect.

The only thing unattractive about her was her cocky personality. I tried to like her, but she kept telling me what an awful gymnast I was, rolling her eyes at me, taunting me, and bragging about how she was going to beat me for the spot.

After practice, as we were all walking to the locker room, Summer came up to me. "Why don't you just quit? There's no need for you to continue competing. The longer you stick around, the more heartache you're gonna have when the coach chooses me instead of you."

"I'm just having a little trouble," I said. "But I'm good, and I'm gonna prove it."

She laughed. "If you crack under pressure here, just imagine how bad you'll do at a meet."

"Hey, I'm not gonna let some girl who twirls her toes around in the air beat me at my game," I said, pulling open my locker so hard it clanged against the one next to it. "I am a gymnast. And I'm going to be a Gym Dawg."

Before Summer could say anything back, the coach came in and asked to see me in her office again. As I followed her, I heard Summer snickering.

Coach Burrows closed the door and motioned for me to have a seat. She perched on the edge of her desk and folded her arms across her chest. "Laurel, I've watched several films of you competing in high school competitions, recreational meets, even a regional tournament. I know you're a great gymnast. But everything I've seen so far in this gym doesn't come close to what's on those tapes." She sighed. "Whatever butterflies you have, you've got to get rid of them. Any doubt you might have about yourself, forget it. You can do this. I want you on this team, but I've got to see better results than what you've been giving me."

"I really do want to be on this team, Coach," I assured her. "I just don't know if I'm good enough."

"I've seen you win meets," she said, returning to her seat behind the desk. "I believe I can make you an even greater athlete than you already are. You can compete on a national level. Eventually you could even get into the Olympics. But you've got to help me out. I need a reason to keep you on this team."

"And I want to give you a reason," I said eagerly.

"Then there's something I want you to do," she said.

"Name it."

"There's a big home football game tomorrow afternoon. I

want you to go there and study the team. See how the players tune out the screaming fans and focus on what they have to do for the team. If you focus on even one player's mental toughness, I believe that will help you stay focused yourself."

"I'll do it," I responded gladly.

"On Monday," she said sternly, "I want to see a different Laurel Shadrach."

"You will, Coach," I promised.

"Come on," I hollered. "You can make it!" I sat in the stands at the Georgia Bulldawgs football game with my dad, all three of my brothers, and seventy-five thousand other fans. Most of us were wearing red, black, and white, the school colors.

In the fourth quarter, with thirty seconds left on the clock, our placekicker, Hanson, was about to try for a field goal. If he made it, our team would win. If not, the Auburn Tigers would beat us.

Everyone in the stands rose to their feet. We stood in silence, not wanting to disturb the kicker. I prayed the ball would make it through the uprights. For some reason, I felt connected to that player. I'd heard he was a freshman and he'd been doing an outstanding job. His field goals had saved the Bulldawgs from defeat before. I hoped he would do it again.

The ball was snapped and placed. Hanson made contact. As the ball sailed into the sky, it veered slightly to the left. We all held our breath. The ball nicked the goalpost and bounced outside. The referees signaled it "no good," and the crowd groaned.

I wanted to weep for the guy. I understood how he felt. I'd been in that position several times, where my score in a gymnastics meet made the difference between win and loss for my team.

Suddenly the crowd started yelling. I looked up and noticed there was a yellow flag on the field. One of the referees had called a foul against the opposing team. The kicker would get another chance!

"Thank You, Lord," I screamed. My family looked at me like I'd lost my mind, but I didn't care.

Hanson's second chance held great symbolic meaning for me. In that moment, it didn't matter that thousands of people were watching. He couldn't let the crowd distract him. He couldn't let what happened on the previous kick upset him. He just had to do his best.

I needed to do that too. I had to give my gymnastics career to the Lord and let Him show His power to make things happen in His name.

Hanson stepped back, held up one hand, then let it fall. When the ball was in place, he stepped up to it and planted his toe firmly against the pigskin.

"It went through!" I screamed. "Thank You, Lord!"

After the game, I practiced at the gym for about an hour, then went to my room to study for midterms.

Payton was there, her rap music blaring. I grabbed my books and decided to find a quieter place to study.

The sorority house had a "study room," but it was more of a gossip chat room than a good place to concentrate. All the classrooms were locked up for the weekend. So I headed for the library.

I found a perfect little place on the third floor. It was the only unoccupied table I could find. The four-person desk beside it was empty too. I sat down and spread my books across the table, excited about getting some good, solid work done.

All of a sudden, an annoying guy stood over me. "Excuse me," he said, "but you're in my seat."

I looked up at him. He looked vaguely familiar. He had short copper-blond hair and beautiful hazel eyes, but I wasn't about to get caught up in his looks.

"There are no assigned seats in the library, and I don't see your name written anywhere on this one. Why don't you take that empty desk?"

He stood there, his strong-looking arms crossed over his muscular chest. "I've been coming here every night since school started," he explained. "I've kind of gotten used to this chair. I know it's an inconvenience, but would it be a big deal for you to move?"

"Look," I said as calmly as I could, "maybe I'm not as attached to this seat as you are, but my stuff is spread out everywhere and I'd rather not move it all. I see no reason why you can't just go study over there."

I pointed to the desk. But we'd been arguing so long, a group of students had set themselves up at there.

He shrugged at me.

I glanced around. The library was packed. The three empty chairs at my table were the only unoccupied seats.

With a long sigh, I stacked my books so they only took up half of the table, and he sat in the empty chair on the opposite side.

I tried to get back to my studying, but the three guys at the desk beside me were talking about the football game. They went on and on about how Hanson should have made the field goal the first time. I wondered how the girl who was with them could possibly concentrate on the textbook in front of her.

"Good thing the other team fouled," said a guy with a goatee and long sideburns.

"Yeah," his friend, who was wearing a fraternity sweatshirt, said. "Otherwise that moron would've cost us the game."

My temper stated rising. I felt a kinship with that kicker, and hearing them talk about him was almost as if they were saying those things about me.

Finally, I turned to them and said, "Hey, if it hadn't been for Hanson, we would have lost the last three games. He's just a freshman, but he's already pulling the team."

They stared at me with blank expressions. I couldn't tell if they agreed with what I was saying, but I wasn't about to let up.

"No game is ever the sole responsibility of the kicker anyway. I mean, we had way too many fumbles, quarterback sacks, interceptions. And our defense wasn't doing anything to stop Auburn. Hanson shouldn't have to win a game all by himself. And yet every score we made today was a field goal."

The girl who was sitting with these guys glanced up from her textbook. I wondered briefly what she thought of my outburst. But I was on a roll, and I wasn't going to stop.

"You think we need a new kicker?" I went on. "Well, Hanson is the only player we should make sure to keep. You know, I find it funny when fans complain about their team. You have no idea what it's like to be down there under all that pressure unless you play sports yourself."

Two of the guys looked at each other and started laughing. The girl turned her attention back to her textbook. But the guy with the hairy face said to me, "I get your point." He gave me a sly grin. "What's your name?"

"Don't worry about my name," I said, offended by his sudden flattery. "You just remember what I said. Next time you're watching a football game, support the whole team. When things go wrong, whoever gets us out of it is a hero, not someone to complain about."

"All right, all right," he said, raising his hands in surrender.

The other boys at the table whistled. The girl looked up at me and grinned. "I totally agree with you. Thanks for putting it in words he can understand."

I smiled at her, then turned back to my books.

"You don't remember me, do you?" the guy at the table said.

"You do look kinda familiar," I replied.

"I helped you pick up your books on the first day of school."

I blushed, recalling how clumsy I'd been. "You were really helpful that day. Thanks."

"You're welcome," he said with a smile. "So, you're a football fan, huh?"

"Yeah, I am," I said.

"I think it's admirable that you stood up for the kicker like that."

I shrugged. "I know how it feels to have a lot riding on your shoulders."

A huge smile lit up his face. "You do?"

"I prayed for his kick to be in God's hands, and—"

"You prayed for him?" the guy said.

"Yeah, I did," I said, starting to feel defensive. "What about it?"

"Hey, I'm not judging. I think that's probably what he needed."

"Maybe," I said, surprised at his response.

The two of us returned to our studying. After a couple of hours of quiet focus, I heard a chair scrape on the floor. I looked up and noticed the guy across from me standing.

"I do come here often," he said. "If you want to, I'd love to share a table with you again sometime."

"Thanks." For some strange reason, I felt giddy inside.

"Maybe I'll see you later?"

"I'd like that."

We smiled at each other. As he walked away I realized we hadn't told each other our names. I was bummed out about that but figured we'd have a chance to introduce ourselves next time.

On Monday morning, I woke up excited. My burdens were light and my yoke was easy.

I spent an hour choosing my outfit for the day and ironing it. Then I spent another hour in the bathroom fixing my hair in a cute style. I had let myself go over the last few weeks because I was so bummed about Branson. It felt good to care about my appearance again.

When I came out of the bathroom, Payton went on and on about how cute I looked. We laughed about it, but she was right. I looked dramatically better than I had in a long time.

Payton was wearing the T-shirt and sweats she had slept in. Her head was covered in curlers. When I vacated the bathroom, she went in.

It was Payton's birthday, so while she was in the bathroom I pulled out the present I had wrapped a few days before and set it on her bed. When she came out and saw it, she smiled.

"How did you know?" she asked.

I smiled without answering. Payton opened the gift and thanked me for the perfume I'd bought her. But her smile soon faded.

"What's wrong?" I asked as she flopped onto her bed.

"My parents forgot my birthday again," she said, a sob catching in her throat. "Every year, when I was growing up, they would wake me up at 12:03 A.M. to give me my presents because that's the time I was born. Last year, they didn't even call me until the next day. I mean, with everything they had going on in their life, I could understand. But two years in a row . . ."

Payton looked like she was going to start crying in her pillow, so I reached under my bed and pulled out the big box her parents had sent me to give to her on her special day. When I handed it to her, she squealed with delight. She ripped the top off the box and found clothes, CDs, and a ton of cosmetics.

After she put all her new stuff away, her smile disappeared and her eyes became sad again.

"Bye," she said in a morose voice as she started out the door. "I'll see you later."

"Wait," I said. "You're not going to class dressed like that, are you?"

97

"Why not?" she said.

"Your parents bought you new clothes, and you're gonna wear those old things?"

She looked down at the wrinkled gray sweats. "So I'm not into dressing up. What's the big deal?"

She shut the door. I prayed that her day would get better. But I was not about to let her unhappiness get me down. I went about my day singing and smiling.

I headed back toward my dorm at the end of the day, still elated. I was confident I'd aced my two midterms, and I'd done better at gymnastics practice than I had in a long time.

When I entered the foyer, I saw the prettiest bouquet of roses I had ever seen sitting in a crystal vase on the dorm monitor's desk. They were a mix of pink, peach, and yellow with lovely green ferns and white baby's breath. "Are these mine?" I teased Judy, the dorm monitor.

"They're for your roommate," Judy said, handing the vase to me. "You can take them to your room if you want."

"Thanks," I said, taking the flowers from the pretty grad student. "It's her birthday today."

"Those roses sure are beautiful," she said. "If they'd stayed here any longer, I might have just kept them for myself." Judy winked and we laughed.

As I took the flowers to our room, I counted eighteen roses, apparently symbolic for Payton's age. I wondered who they were from.

When I got to our room, I almost lost everything as I tried to twist the doorknob while holding the vase and all my books.

"You shouldn't try to be Superwoman," I heard Jewels's voice behind me. "Just put something down, open the door, then come out and get the rest."

Her advice made a lot of sense, although I would have liked it more if she'd have just helped me for a change. But at least she was talking to me again. That was good enough.

Besides, I was having such a great day, I decided not to let her spoil it.

"Thank you, Jewels," I said, taking her advice and setting down my books. I took the vase in and put it on Payton's nightstand, then came back for the rest of my stuff. I tried to shut the door before Jewels could ask about the flowers, but I wasn't quick enough.

"Nice roses," she said, following me into the room. "Are you and Branson getting back together?"

"These are for Payton," I explained as I set my books on the desk.

"Well, let's see who they're from." She reached for the card that was clipped onto a pink plastic holder stuck into the bouquet.

"No!" I yelled.

She glared up at me. "Fine. Whatever." She left the room in a huff, going through the adjoining bathroom to her room.

I sat at my desk to study, peeking up once in a while and staring at the card, wondering who the flowers might be from.

The minute Payton came in, I pointed to the roses. She looked at them, opened the card, and tossed it into the wastebasket.

"Who are they from?" I asked, dying to know.

"Dakari," she said without emotion.

Jewels came bursting into the room, and she and Payton started arguing about Dakari. I wondered if Jewels was feeling a bruised ego because Dakari had sent Payton flowers, which maybe meant he was trying to move back into Payton's life. I could tell Payton didn't want to rub it in her face, but Jewels was asking for it.

Not wanting to get involved in their squabble, I snuck into the bathroom and took a long shower.

When I came back into the room, Jewels was gone. But I saw a gift-wrapped box on Payton's bed.

"What's that?" I asked with a grin. "A birthday present from Jewels?"

"Of course not," Payton snarled. "The dorm monitor just asked her to give it to me."

"Aren't you going to open it?" I asked.

She shrugged. "I guess I can, now that *she's* gone." Payton opened the card. "It's from Tad."

Man, I thought. *Having one ex-boyfriend is bad enough. I can't imagine having two!*

Tad had given Payton a Christian book.

"You are so lucky," I said. "You got so many birthday presents from people who care about you."

"I don't give a rip about all this stuff," she grumbled, wadding up the wrapping paper. "I have too much going on in my life right now to think about presents."

"Let's take your mind off things," I suggested. "How about letting me take you out to dinner for your birthday?"

"No thanks," she said, kicking off her shoes. "I don't want to do anything right now."

I couldn't just let her sit there and mope. Somehow I convinced her to go out to dinner with me. On the way there we chatted about our insecurities, guy issues, our spiritual walks. We commiserated about all the pressure we were both under but reassured each other that God was with us, helping us stand.

After getting all that out into the open, we were able to have a great time at the restaurant.

The walk back to our dorm room was heavenly. The sky was calm and blue. And the conversation was honest. Payton finally let my good mood rub off on her. As we neared the dorm, Payton stopped and looked at me. "Thanks for being pushy with me earlier. I really appreciate you going the extra mile, caring about me, and helping me with my problems."

"We've both got to take life day by day," I told her. "Sometimes minute by minute. The Holy Spirit lives in you and me, and we can do all things through Him. If you choose to have a good day, you can. It's not what happens to you that's important; it's how you respond to what happens to you. For me, I want to be happy. And I'm finally thinking I can."

looking, not finding

i don't understand. I've been studying. Why am I getting Cs? I was sitting in the library, at the same table where I'd met the handsome stranger, trying to figure out where I'd gone wrong with my schoolwork and whether that cute guy would show up at the library again.

As if reading my thoughts, he walked up to the table. "Mind if I sit down?" he asked politely.

"This time you're asking my permission?" I said, giving him a hard time. "How come?"

"I don't know. Trying to be a gentleman, I guess. That or I'm just a sucker for a pretty face."

I felt my cheeks blushing. "Go ahead," I said, trying to sound casual. As he sat, he looked at my psych paper with the C grade.

"Guess I'm not the only one struggling with psychology."

His comment made me feel like we were allies in a common struggle.

"I only got a B on that last test," he complained.

So we weren't in the same boat after all. I would have loved a B.

We talked about the questions he'd missed on the test and then we discussed the ones I'd gotten wrong. We chatted about our other classes too. I discovered he had a good sense of humor. He was also sweet and encouraging.

"It's just midterms," he assured me. "You still have time to pull up your grades."

I knew he was right. I determined to study harder and make sure I scored better on my next test.

When I got back to the dorm, I found a big commotion going on in the lobby. Mandelyn and Jill came rushing up to me, panting. They were both talking at the same time, and I couldn't understand either of them.

"A girl from the dorm," Jill said between gulps of breath.

"She's missing," Mandelyn added. "Freshman. Long brown hair. Soft hazel eyes."

"Her name's Worth Zachary. Do you know her?"

I vaguely recognized the name but couldn't place her.

Mandelyn gave me some of the flyers she'd been handing out around the campus. "We're gonna go pass out some more of these," she said. "Want to join us?"

"Yeah, in a minute," I said. "I've got to drop off these books first."

As I hurried to my room, I prayed every step of the way. *Lord, please help us find this girl. Keep her safe. Help her not to be scared. Thank You, God.*

As I said, "Amen," I hoped with all my heart that Worth was OK.

When I burst into my room and found Payton there, I talked to her in the same out-of-breath way Mandelyn and Jill had spoken to me.

"Slow down," my roommate said. "I can't understand a word you're saying."

"A girl is missing," I said, handing her one of the flyers.

"Someone from our dorm. A freshman, just like us. Oh, Payton, I hope she's OK."

I dropped my books and the rest of the flyers, and the two of us hugged. I could tell Payton cared just as much as I did about this girl we didn't know. I started to go through the bathroom to tell our suite mates, but before I reached the door, I heard a sharp sound like glass shattering. I shoved open the door.

I found Jewels sitting on top of Anna, swatting her with a pillow. Bits of glass covered the carpet in one corner where, apparently, a drinking glass had been knocked off the bedside table by a flying pillow. The two of them looked ridiculous. With Anna's larger size, she could easily flick Jewels off her. But she wasn't doing that. I stood there in shock, staring at the ludicrous sight.

"You fat, ugly, no-good rodent!" Jewels screamed. "I'm sick of you whining all the time, as if anybody cares that you're hurting. So you didn't make it into a sorority. That's all in the past now, so just get over it and move on."

Anna was sobbing so hard she couldn't speak.

"I hate you," Jewels said. "You're nothing."

I raced over and gave Jewels a shove, pushing her off of Anna. "What are you doing? Why are you being so mean?"

Anna scampered into a corner. I didn't want to leave her alone, but I needed to get Jewels out of there. "Let's go outside and get some fresh air, OK?" I suggested.

Jewels scowled at me, then pranced out the door.

I wished Payton would step in and do something for Anna. But she'd made her position clear on the first day we arrived at this place. Anna had sided with Jewels when she suggested I request a roommate who wasn't black, and Payton hadn't said a word to either one of them since.

"I'll be back," I said weakly to Anna, then ran after Jewels. Talking to her was like talking to a brick wall, but I tried anyway. I could tell she wasn't listening to a word I said.

"I don't know why I waste my time with you," I said, throwing my hands up in the air.

"I don't know why you never see my side," she countered.

"You were on top of her, for goodness sake!"

"So what?" Jewels said, crossing her arms. "The cow deserved it."

"Why do you have to call her names? Can't you see how much that hurts her? You're tearing her apart. One of these days she's gonna snap."

Jewels snorted. "She just cries to get attention."

"Jewels, you need to start treating other people like you want to be treated."

She eyed me with suspicion. "Oh, you're a good one to talk."

"What's that supposed to mean?" I asked.

"You took the pledge class president job, even though you knew how much I wanted it."

"Oh, so that's what this is all about, huh? Look, I was voted in. I didn't run for that position. I never asked for it. It's not my fault you were late and acted like a snot to everybody."

"You should have turned it down," she seethed.

"Well, I didn't."

Her eyes narrowed. "Which is exactly my point. You take things that other people want, and you don't give a thought to how they feel. So don't go telling me to treat people like I want to be treated because you're no different from me."

I wanted to dispute her comment but couldn't think of a good reply.

"We're exactly alike, you and I. I'm just more honest about my faults. You hide behind all that Christianity stuff, but you're not fooling anybody."

"That's crazy!" I hollered. "I'm sorry you're upset about the pledge class president thing, but that's in the past now, so just get over it and move on."

Jewels raised her eyebrows at me, and I immediately wished I could take back the words. They were exactly what Jewels had said to Anna about not being in a sorority. *"Get over it and move on."* Maybe I hadn't been considerate enough of Jewels's feelings.

"Just forget it," my irate friend grumbled as she turned on her heels and stomped away.

Lord, I prayed as I watched her leave, *help me search myself and find where I need improvement. I'm struggling with so much right now. But You've given me friends who are struggling too. Please work in my heart and let my life be a witness to Your power in me.*

A couple of days later, my dad and my middle brother, Lance, came to the University of Georgia campus to attend a football game with me. I was so excited!

Lance was in the eleventh grade, and he was the starting quarterback on the high school team. He was a major Georgia Tech fan and had dreams of playing ball for them. He wasn't as smart academically as my youngest brother, Luke. But last year he'd maintained a 3.5 GPA, and that was just good enough to get into Tech.

"How's Lance doing in school this year?" I asked my dad while my brother was talking to a friend at the end of our row.

"Not that well," Dad told me. "The gambling and drinking problems you found out about over the summer have been catching up with him."

Lance joined us, and Dad left to get some refreshments.

"I heard your grades have slipped," I said right up front.

He looked shocked at my abruptness, then gave me a shrug. "Yeah. So what?"

"You'd better start buckling down if you want to be out there on that field next year," I said, pointing to the players who were warming up.

"I don't need Miss 4.0 trying to preach to me, OK?" he grumbled.

I shook my head. "Hey, I was never a 4.0."

"Three-nine. Three-eight. Same thing."

"Yeah, well, I've been getting Cs here."

His eyes widened. "You?"

"Yeah," I confessed. "And I've been studying."

He chuckled. "Yeah, right. You're in a sorority now. I know what you've been doing—partying, having a good time."

"I have been to a few parties," I admitted, "but I've been working too."

"Well, I'm not planning to come to this stupid school anyway, so you can stop ragging on me. I've already applied to Georgia Tech. You wait and see. When we play the Bull-dawgs two years from now . . ."

"What?" I asked, calling my little brother's bluff.

"When I'm on the team, it's gonna be something."

"Yeah, OK." I drilled my knuckles into his forehead like I used to do when I was living at home. Man, I missed him. He and I had a great relationship growing up. I loved all three of my brothers, but Lance and I seemed to always be on the same level. Liam, my oldest younger brother, had a great walk with God. Luke, the baby, was the brainy one who could always make me laugh. But Lance was on the wild side. He liked to have fun, like me. And sometimes that fun got him into trouble. Like it had for me a few times. So he understood me in a way my other brothers didn't. Sometimes I thought he knew me better than I knew myself.

I wanted to tell him how much I missed him, but I knew he'd just shrug me off. So I gave him a big hug instead.

The game started just as Dad came back with cardboard trays full of hot dogs and sodas. Our team was playing Florida, and they had a really cute quarterback named Jett Phillips. He was a Heisman trophy candidate, the leading passer in the nation, and Lance really admired him.

Payton came up to us with her father and her brother, Perry, who was two years younger than she was. We intro-duced our family members, and everybody hit it off. Payton even introduced Jett Phillips to us, which absolutely thrilled Lance.

On Monday morning, when I returned to my dorm after working out at the gym, I was surprised to see news cameras all over the place.

When I walked up to the front door, a police officer stopped me and asked my name. When I told him who I was, he checked a printout on a clipboard. "You're clear," he said, then let me pass.

"What's going on?" I asked.

"Only students who live in this dorm are allowed to enter," he said firmly.

I wanted to ask why, but his gruff demeanor told me I wasn't going to get any details out of him.

I swallowed hard and blinked back tears when I saw Jill, Mandelyn, and some other girls gathered at a table in the corner of the foyer, crying.

I sat in an empty chair near Mandelyn. "Is this about Worth Zachary?" I asked.

"She was found dead," Jill said, choking back sobs.

"A police detective came by the dorm this morning," Mandelyn added. "He told us that Worth went on a date with an older man from Athens. She ended up in a trash bin behind a service station!"

"I told her not to go out with a stranger," Jill said, flopping her tear-streaked face onto her crossed arms on the table.

"Don't blame yourself," an older man with short dark hair and a pinched nose said. He turned to me. "I'm a psychologist," he explained. "The police asked me to come in and give you girls some tips on how to handle a situation like Ms. Zachary found herself in." His eyes connected with each one of us as he handed a slip of paper to every girl at the table. "Here is a list of places you can go to, to talk about your grief and pain and confusion." He touched Jill's shoulder and she looked up at him through clouded eyes. "It's not your fault. When a person gets it into her mind to do something, no one is responsible for that decision but her."

Jill didn't reply, but I could tell she felt a little bit comforted.

The psychologist turned his attention back to the group. "Now, there are some things you can do to keep yourselves safe. Before you go on a date with someone you don't know, ask for a driver's license or student ID. Let other people know where you're going. Write down the license plate number of the guy's car, and make sure someone sees you leave so that person will have a description in case anything happens to you. Try to stay in public places and always take your own money. You might even want to carry mace."

I knew he was giving us good advice, and I wondered if Worth's death could have been prevented if she'd done those things. But at that moment, the only thing I could really think about was the status of her relationship with God. I didn't know the girl well, so I had no way of telling whether or not she knew the Lord. It was tragic that her earthly life was over, but it would be even more tragic if she didn't know Jesus Christ as her Savior.

I recalled meeting Worth Zachary at the soda machine a few weeks ago. We talked about trivial things, like school and grades and sports. But now I wished I'd asked, *"Do you know God? Have you let Jesus Christ into your heart? Is the Holy Spirit living inside of you?"*

But I had said none of those things to her. I'd been too wrapped up in myself, not wanting to step outside my comfort zone and speak about eternal things to a stranger. Now she was gone, and I'd never be able to say anything to her again in this world.

Lord, I prayed, *forgive me. Help me be bold enough to tell everyone I meet about You.*

As I prayed for Worth Zachary's soul, I thanked God for helping me gain perspective once again. Boyfriends and sororities and gymnastics teams and school grades had seemed like such a big deal. But I knew I needed to stay focused on God. He was the most important thing in my life, and I needed to start acting like it.

"I'll never find the right dress," I whined to my mom as I stared at a store full of wrong ones.

The fall formal was coming up, and I wanted to look perfect, or at least the best I could. But after shopping at every clothing store within ten miles of the college campus, I hadn't been able to find a single dress I liked. When I'd called my mother to complain, she dropped everything to take me shopping at the outlet mall.

I hadn't meant to impose on my mom. She was busy enough taking care of my brothers, helping Dad with the church, and doing all the charitable activities she was involved in. And I was in college now. I needed to learn to take care of myself, to act like an adult. But talking to Mom about my insecurities, and hearing her combat every negative thing I said about myself with something positive, made me feel good inside.

Shopping with my mom for the perfect dress had seemed like a great way to lighten my heart after all the catastrophes at school. But when it appeared as though I'd never find the right dress for my first college ball, I started feeling like I shouldn't bother going at all.

Then I heard my mom utter sweet words from behind me. "Laurel, honey, I think this might be the one."

I turned around quickly, hoping she was right. When I saw the gown she held up for my inspection, it was like a gift from God. I mean, it was just a dress, but I had really been praying that I would find the right gown, one that would help me feel confident about myself.

God had heard my plea. Not only did the peach satin gown fit me like it had been tailor-made, but it was in my price range, and it was the only one on the rack in that size. I knew that angels had placed it there especially for me, because when I was looking at that rack a few moments before, I hadn't even noticed it.

Maybe I was exaggerating about God's intervention a little. But the Lord's timing is always perfect, and He does delight in answering our prayers.

When I walked out of the fitting room wearing the special peach gown, my mother gasped and told me how beautiful I looked. I had never really longed for her approval in that way before, but after being away from her, I deeply missed hearing her words of affirmation on a consistent basis. I spun around, letting the hem of the dress fly through the air as I twirled.

I hugged my mom tight. All of a sudden I didn't even care about the dance anymore because my perfect moment had already happened.

After the dress was purchased and hanging in the back of Mom's minivan, we ventured to our favorite place, the Christian bookstore. Whenever I was going through drama in my life, that's where Mom took me. "There has to be a book in here to minister to where you are right now," she always said, "to help you grow, to help you heal, to help you seek God in your circumstances."

I thanked the Lord that my mother knew me so well. She understood, without my having to say anything, that I was more fragile than I had ever been. After only a couple of hours of shopping with me, she had picked up on my issues and knew I needed some help.

Mom asked the bookstore manager for assistance in finding something that dealt with self-esteem. He led us to a book by Dannah Gresh called *Secret Keeper: The Delicate Power of Modesty*. I had read her book *And the Bride Wore White: The Seven Secrets to Sexual Purity*. I liked the author's style, and that book had really helped me cement my decision to stay sexually pure until marriage.

"Thanks, Mom," I said as we climbed into the car with our purchase. "I'm going to read a chapter of this right before I go to my dance."

"I'm sure there are some great ideas in there," she said, "but I also want you to know that I love you. Your dad loves you. Your brothers love you. You should never feel apprehensive about who you are or doubt how much you're loved."

"I know," I said, smiling.

"And if insecurity mounts, just think about Christ and the price He paid for you. When you realize that your worth is His worth, you can't help but feel confident."

I stood near the convention center door while my date, J. D. Braden, went to get us some soda. I couldn't stop staring at the dance floor, where Jewels and Branson were dancing up a storm. Somehow, she had managed to snag *my* Branson as her date!

The same emotions I'd felt when I saw him under the steps with Brittany in high school came rushing back. Though he wasn't kissing Jewels, I knew it was only a matter of time before they went down that road.

I hadn't come right out and asked Branson to take me to the ball, but I'd hinted at him once when I ran into him at the frat house, and he'd completely blown me off. I knew Jewels was mad at me about being pledge class president and coming down so hard on her when she got into it with Anna. But I didn't think she'd be so conniving as to steal the man she knew I loved.

J. D. was a nice guy, and he always behaved like a perfect gentleman with me. He was president of his pledge class as well, which was how we'd met. But I hadn't really noticed him until he invited me to the ball. Partly out of spite, and partly hoping Branson would ask me and I could tell him he was too late, I accepted J. D.'s offer. But Branson hadn't asked.

When she noticed me staring at her, Jewels grabbed Branson's hands and placed them right on her bottom, where her expensive silver metallic dress clung tightly to her curves. She gave me a smug grin.

When she went out with Payton's ex-boyfriend Dakari, I had been a little irritated with Jewels. But now, when it was *my* old boyfriend being flirted with, I was really mad.

J. D. came back with two cans of soda, and I took one of them, but otherwise I ignored him. I glared at Jewels as if I hoped my stare would make her leave his side. But she continued to stand there with him, arm in arm, face-to-face, swaying her hips to the music.

At the end of the dance, the two of them returned to their table. When she nuzzled her lips into his neck, I couldn't take any more. I sauntered up to Jewels and whispered in her ear. "Why?"

She just laughed at me.

"Why!" I screamed.

Branson stared at me in shock. So did most of the people in the room. But I didn't care.

"You accused me of taking something you wanted," I said to Jewels. "Well, it looks like you've got something I want now. So we're even. Now you can just quit making a spectacle of yourself and get out of my face."

"Why should I?" she asked, a teased eyebrow raised in defiance.

I lunged at her like I was going to take her head off. She dodged me, and I went sprawling to the tile floor. I heard a ripping sound and realized that I'd torn my beautiful peach dress.

I was acting like a nutcase. No wonder Branson didn't want me anymore. I wasn't too fond of myself at that moment.

Julie Anne grabbed her sister and me by the arms and led us into the hallway. Jewels loudly defended herself, and I defended myself right back.

"Calm down," Julie Anne said when we were alone. "While you two were going at each other in there, something dramatic happened at your dorm."

"Yeah, yeah, we know," Jewels said, obviously eager to get back on the dance floor with my man. "Worth Zachary's dead."

"Not that," she said, shaking her head. "I just got word that there's an ambulance at your dorm."

"Oh, my gosh," I said. "What happened?"

"All I know is that they're taking somebody to the hospital. You guys had better get over there right away."

We didn't even go back to tell our dates we were leaving. Jewels headed straight for her Mustang and I hopped in beside her. Neither of us said a word during the ten-minute drive.

The sound of wailing sirens grew louder the closer we got to the dorm. Just before we reached the building, a speeding ambulance passed us in the opposite direction.

"I sure hope that's not Anna," Jewels moaned. To my surprise, she seemed genuinely concerned about her roommate.

When we got to the dorm, we saw a bunch of girls standing around in groups on the lawn. We tried asking people for details, but no one seemed to know anything.

"Where's Payton?" I kept asking.

"Have you seen Anna?" Jewels asked everyone.

Our hysterics escalated when we had no success getting answers. We were looking, not finding.

holding
life steady

"W e've got to get up to our room," I said to Jewels. She looked as petrified as I felt.

All kinds of thoughts tumbled through my mind. What had happened in our dorm? Burglary, rape, kidnapping, fire? Did someone pass out or get shot? Who had just been driven away by ambulance to the hospital? Was it someone I knew? Could it be Payton or Anna?

We tried to enter our building, but the campus police weren't letting anyone through.

"I've got an idea," I said, grabbing Jewels by the arm and heading around the side of the dorm.

"Where are we going?" Jewels asked.

"To our room."

She blinked at me. "The front door's that way."

I rolled my eyes. "Our window is this way."

"What are we going to do? Bust the glass?"

"Wouldn't be the first time," I said with a grin, remembering my first day on campus when Payton's ex-boyfriend Dakari put his fist through the window trying to hit her other ex-boyfriend Tad.

When we rounded the corner of the building, I stopped. I couldn't even see our window. People were crowded around it like there was a free concert going on in our room.

"What is everybody staring at?" Jewels wondered out loud.

"Hey," I yelled, trying to get someone's attention. "Does anybody know what's going on?" A few girls turned their heads briefly, then refocused their attention inside.

Judy, the dorm monitor, pulled away from the crowd and came up to us with a sad and worried face. "Girls," she said, her voice cracking with emotion, "I'm afraid it's Anna."

Tears stung my eyes. *Lord,* I prayed, *please let my friend be OK.*

"You two had better get inside," Judy said. "If the press finds out you're her roommates, they'll swoop down on you like vultures."

"Can't you tell us what happened?" Jewels whispered as Judy ushered us toward the back of the building.

"Is Payton all right?" I asked.

"Payton's fine," Judy assured me.

"What happened to Anna?" Jewels persisted.

Judy led us to a back door with a maintenance sign on it. She looked both ways to make sure no one saw us, then dug through her pockets for a key ring loaded with keys. After locating the right one, she rushed us inside and re-locked the door.

Judy sighed, looking at us with a pained expression. "Anna tried to commit suicide tonight."

"What?" I squealed.

I turned to Jewels, expecting to see a horrified expression on her face. But she just stood there with dry eyes, apparently unmoved by what our dorm monitor had just said.

116

I turned back to Judy, my knees trembling. "You said *tried*, right?"

"She was alive when the ambulance left," Judy explained, "but she was very weak."

"Is she going to make it?" I choked out.

"We're not sure."

I hugged Judy and thanked her for telling us the news.

"Come on," she said, heading down the narrow corridor.

When we turned a corner and stepped into the hall that led to our dorm room, I saw several girls with mops and buckets and sponges in their hands going in and out of my room and Jewels's. Their jeans were soaked and their faces looked weary.

Did Anna try to drown herself in the bathtub? I wondered.

I hurried down the hallway, tears flooding my eyes. "Thanks, you guys," I whispered to the girls with the mops. Jewels came up slowly behind me, still not saying a word.

I entered my dorm room, stepping carefully to avoid slipping on the layer of water that covered the floor. I glanced around. Besides the wet floor, everything looked just the way I'd left it. Payton wasn't there, but I noticed a note lying on her bed. I picked it up and unfolded it.

Dear Laurel,

    I'm sorry I can't be here to tell you what happened in person, but my dad came by and insisted I go home with him.

    After you left for your dance, I decided to take a quick nap before my party. When I woke up a few minutes later, I heard water running. I got up and went to the bathroom. When I opened the door, I found Anna lying in the tub, unconscious, with the water still running. A handful of pills were lying on the floor just below her right arm.

    I screamed for help and someone called 911. Thankfully, Anna was still alive when the ambulance came.

    The paramedics said Anna's going to be OK, so I guess I got to her in time to save her. But I don't feel very good about it. I knew for a long time that she was hurting, but I refused to get involved or try to help her. If I'd shown her friendship and kindness before, maybe she wouldn't have done what she did today.

I hope you and Anna can forgive me.

Just as the paramedics were loading Anna into the ambulance, my dad came. He said Judy called him. I wanted to stay and help clean up the water mess in our room, but he convinced me to go home. You can call me there if you want.

Payton

None of this made sense. Sure, Anna was a little overweight. And she hadn't been accepted into a sorority. She didn't get the attention of the guys like Jewels did, and she didn't have perfect grades. But she still had so much to live for. She was young, intelligent, and humble. She had goals and dreams. I remembered a lengthy conversation we'd had once about her wanting to become a pharmacist. She'd even interned at a drugstore in her hometown. Her heart was pure and earnest. The world needed more folks like Anna around.

I wished I hadn't been so focused on trying to change Jewels. I should have spent more time building Anna's self-esteem instead. Perhaps I could have helped her believe in herself. Even more important, I wished I'd have talked to her more about Christ, so she could find hope in Him.

I punched my hand into the wall. I didn't make a dent in the plaster or anything, but my fist turned crimson and started to throb. That just made my tension rise.

I shot out into the hallway. "Anybody seen Jewels?" I asked, a dozen emotions churning in my heart.

"I think she went to the lobby," one of the girls in the bucket brigade answered.

"Thanks," I said, then raced off to find her.

Jewels was sitting in an overstuffed chair in the corner, her head in her hands. I ran up to her.

"This is your fault, you know," I railed. "If you hadn't

nagged Anna so much, she wouldn't have wanted to kill herself. All you had to do was say something nice to her once in a while. But you kept telling her she was nothing until she started to believe it. You don't care about anyone besides yourself, do you? Well, I hate to tell you this, but the world does not revolve around you."

Jewels finally looked up at me, and I saw deep despair in her eyes. Tears streamed down her cheeks, falling in little drops from her chin. Filled with compassion, I knelt beside my suite mate and she cried in my arms.

I suddenly felt bad for the harsh words I'd said. I needed to lift my friend up, not tear her down like she'd done to Anna. "It's going to be OK," I whispered in her ear.

God gave me an opportunity to share the gospel with Jewels. I told her that Christ died for her sins, and if she would accept Him into her heart, she could be saved. I couldn't tell if she was understanding what I said, but I felt good about telling her anyway.

"How can you believe that God answers prayer?" Jewels asked in a sincere voice. "What about Anna?"

"God woke Payton up from her nap before it was too late to get to Anna," I explained. "He sent Payton to save her."

Jewels's eyes brimmed with tears.

"He's working in your heart too, Jewels. I can tell."

She looked all around, as if she were uncomfortable. I could tell God was calling her to Himself. She wouldn't have peace until she gave in to Him.

Another tear dropped down her cheek. I sensed that she was close to giving her life to Christ. But I didn't want to force her. I waited for her to ask me what was next, but she didn't. I prayed silently that God would keep knocking on the door of her heart.

At that moment I felt pure peace in my heart. My world had turned upside down, but I was finally putting God first in my life. Hope had come into a hopeless situation, and I was able to smile in spite of my pain.

When Jewels and I returned to our rooms, the water had all been mopped up. The girls who had pitched in to help had done an outstanding job. The place looked cleaner than I'd ever seen it.

"I can't stay here," Jewels told me. "I think I'll go to the sorority house and spend the night with my sister."

"I'll be praying for you," I said as she walked out the door.

After Jewels left, I collapsed onto my bed. The room was completely quiet. No girls chatted in the hallway. No suite mates bickered in the next room. My roommate wasn't snoring in the bed next to mine.

In the silence I prayed that God would help Anna recover from her physical pain. I asked Him to help her heal emotionally as well. I prayed that Jewels would turn to Christ in her guilt and that He would free her from it.

I prayed for hours, unable to sleep. I focused on listening to whatever God might want to say to me in this crisis. What did I need to hear? What message did He have for me?

About two in the morning, it dawned on me. God wanted me to keep praying to Him in the midst of my circumstances. And not just for myself but for my friends too.

I got up and walked over to Payton's bed. I laid my hands on her pillow and prayed out loud for her. "Lord, give my roommate sweet, sweet slumber tonight and cover her in Your love." My voice felt small in the quiet, empty room. But I knew the words were ascending to a big, powerful God.

I strode into the bathroom and prayed over the tub. "Lord, may Your Spirit reign freely in this place. Drive out the demons of despair."

Then I went into my suite mates' room. I lifted my hands as high as I could. "Holy Spirit, fill this place. Dwell inside the hearts of those who live here."

Feeling that my job was complete, I returned to my bed,

wrapped in the warmth of God's peace. But I was still unable to sleep. I knew there was something else I needed to do.

I peered over at Payton's empty bed. Feeling a strong need to check on her to see if she was OK, I looked at the clock on my bedside table. I hated to impose on her at 3 A.M., but I simply had to hear her voice.

I picked up the phone and dialed.

"Hey, girl, it's me, Laurel," I said. "Hope I didn't wake you up."

"I wasn't sleeping," she said. Her voice sounded strained but not like she'd been asleep.

"Thanks for leaving the note. I'm glad you were able to save Anna."

After a long pause, she said, "I was almost too late."

"But you got to her in time. I wish I could have been there."

"I'm glad you weren't," she said. "Seeing Anna like that . . ." Her voice trailed off.

"It must have been awful. But I'm glad you were there. I'm even more glad that God was there with you and Anna."

"Do you think He's really with her, even though she doesn't believe in Him?"

"Yeah, I do," I said. "And who knows? Maybe God will use this incident to bring her to Christ."

"Maybe," Payton said, although she didn't sound convinced. "So, where was that no-good sorority sister of yours? You know, I feel like yanking out all that precious red hair of hers strand by strand."

I couldn't believe the anger and hostility I was hearing. I wanted to talk Payton out of that attitude. But the truth was, I'd had some of those same feelings myself before I spent some time with God. I was still mad at Jewels, but I knew she was truly sorry for the way she'd treated Anna.

"How could God let something like this happen?" Payton wailed. "Why didn't He do something to stop it?"

"He did," I said, realizing that Payton's anger wasn't just directed at Jewels. She was also mad at God and maybe herself as well. "He used you to help Anna."

Her anger subsided, and we talked until almost dawn. We finally decided to try to get some sleep, although we both knew we wouldn't get much.

Life can be like a typhoon sometimes, I thought as I lay on my bed. *Crazy, sporadic, hectic, and horrible, even deadly. But in the midst of all that, the Lord can restore order if we choose to let Him lead.*

I thanked God for my Christian roommate. Anna and Jewels were not yet part of God's family. But I believed the Lord wanted to use Payton and me to help them. If all this drama was leading up to that, I would be extremely happy about it all.

The following weekend, my dad came to the college to be a guest speaker for Youth Day. In an auditorium full of hundreds of students, he spoke about having a purpose and knowing God's plan for our lives.

As I sat there listening to him, I kept wondering if I was doing what God had called me to do. How could I make sure I was doing what He wanted me to do?

I knew the Lord had a plan for me. But instead of trying to figure it out, I'd been stressing over all the stuff that had been going wrong in my life. I didn't know how much more disaster I could take.

After the talk, my dad and I went to the Cracker Barrel, where Mom joined us. The warm, familiar restaurant felt cozy after being out in the cool late-October air.

"Laurel, you're shaking," Mom said when she saw me walk in the door. She wrapped her arms around me. Dad took off his jacket and placed it around my shoulders. I reveled in their attentiveness.

While we ate our dinner, we talked about all the things

that had been happening in my life. After discussing the girl who was murdered and Anna's attempt to kill herself, Dad asked how things were going between me and Branson.

"I don't know what I'm going to do about that," I said. "He told me to leave him alone, that he wants me out of his life for good."

"Really?" Mom sounded happy about that, but she didn't want to rub it in.

Dad swallowed a bite of pork roast. "Well, you have a lot of other things to focus your energy on besides that young man."

"We've been praying for your future mate since the day you were born," Mom reminded me. "You can trust that God will give you the right guy in His time."

I was glad that both of my parents had a strong relationship with the Lord.

After dinner, my parents dropped me off at the dorm. As I watched them drive away, part of me wanted to leave with them. Truth was, part of them would always be with me.

Judy, the dorm monitor, kept us girls up-to-date on Anna's progress. I'd been lifting Anna up in prayer continually and was thankful to hear she was recovering. A few times Payton and I talked about visiting her in the hospital, but we never did. I guess we both felt guilty for not doing more to stop the incident from happening in the first place. We were also extremely busy with schoolwork and social activities.

My sorority was planning a fun Halloween party, and I'd really been looking forward it. I looked in the mirror and smiled. I was wearing the prettiest antebellum dress I had ever seen. I thought I looked just like Scarlett O'Hara from *Gone with the Wind*. I even had the wide-brimmed hat, long white gloves, a pearl necklace, and a fake diamond ring.

"You don't see anything wrong with that getup?" Payton asked.

"Why are you being so negative?" I asked. "It's Halloween. Have some fun."

"I can't have fun knowing you and your little white girlfriends are all prancing around looking like you own a plantation."

I suddenly realized what her problem was. I was dressed up like a Southern belle during the time in our country's history when white people owned black slaves. I sighed. Why did everything have to be racial with her?

"It's just a costume," I said. "It's not like I'm wearing a pointy white sheet over my head."

Her nostrils flared. "You really don't understand why that outfit offends me, do you?"

I sat on the bed beside her. "No, I really don't. I mean, you're not a slave. Your parents weren't slaves. The Civil War ended a long time ago. Slavery was abolished, and everyone has equal rights now. What difference does it make what happened years ago?"

I could tell my words had pierced Payton's heart. But I really wanted to understand her.

"I had to do a paper about a hero for one of my classes last week," Payton said, her voice softening a little. "I picked Rosa Parks, the black woman who was arrested for refusing to give up her seat on a bus to a white man. You know, it was only about fifty years ago that colored people couldn't use the same water fountains as white folks or go into the same restaurants. They couldn't even try on shoes in the same stores where white women shopped, wearing dresses like the one you have on now. My ancestors had to trace their kids' feet on paper bags and take the drawings to the shoe store to see which shoes matched. Then they prayed the shoes they bought would fit because they weren't allowed to take them back."

"Payton, I'm just going to a sorority party. Everyone is dressing like this. It's nothing personal."

"Well, I'm sorry, but this sort of thing just makes me

mad. I've tried not to get agitated about the past, but it isn't easy. Can't y'all just wear normal dresses? Why does everybody have to dress up as a Southern belle?"

"People wear costumes on Halloween. It's a fun tradition."

"Well, that costume is offensive to me."

"I'm sorry," I said, returning to the mirror. "But you really need to get past that. Yes, slavery was wrong. But I'm not condoning prejudice just by wearing this. It's a beautiful dress, and I feel like a graceful, charming woman in it. Now, if you want my advice—"

Payton stood abruptly. "I don't need any advice from you!" She picked up her purse and stormed out of the room. After she slammed the door, I sat on my bed, but the hoopskirt flew up and practically hit me in the nose.

I maneuvered into a lying position across my bed, the hoopskirt sticking straight up in the air. "Lord," I prayed, "forgive me for offending Payton. Help me to understand her better so I can be more sensitive to her. I only want to say and do the things You want me to say and do."

———

As my sorority sisters and I sipped lemon-ginger tea and mouthwatering pastries, we listened to the state superintendent, who was also an Alpha Gamma Delta, Ms. Kathleen Tinny. She was very inspiring. She told us how she had worked her way up from being an elementary schoolteacher to personally assisting the governor of Georgia. I'll never forget the last words she said to us. "Life might not always take you where you want to go," she said, "but if you know your final destination, you won't stop until you get there. Ladies, never give up on your dreams."

I was deeply moved. I felt God had sent her to encourage me personally. Even with the bumps I'd received in my life, I was moving forward. I was holding life steady.

t e n

having
no fun

i feel like I'm sitting with a bunch of snobs.

I sat at a large round table at the sorority Halloween party, my Scarlett O'Hara gown billowing out all around me. About 120 girls were sipping lemon-ginger tea from delicate china cups decorated with pink rosebuds. None of them seemed the least bit motivated by the dynamic speech the state superintendent was giving. I was so fired up I felt like standing and cheering. But most of the other girls were slouched in their chairs. Some were talking and a few were even yawning.

Jill, who was sitting to my right, leaned in my direction. "Enough talking already," she said under her breath. "When do we get to eat?"

Maybe I hadn't joined the right sorority after all.

A few seconds later, Jewels, who sat on my left, whispered, "All this pep talk stuff may work for the losers around here, but I just need to find a great man with a big expense account, get married, and have a bunch of kids."

I shot her a quick glance, hoping she'd be quiet so I could listen to the speech.

"Hey, don't take this wrong," she continued, not getting my hint, "but with this face and body, I won't have any trouble finding a man who will give me everything I desire."

The two sorority sisters sitting on the other side of Jewels frowned at her. The closest one looked like she was about to lash out at her, so I grabbed Jewels's elbow and asked her to go to the ladies' room with me.

"Why did you do that?" she whined when we entered the little room. "I was in the middle of talking."

"You know, Jewels, you really need to think before you speak your mind."

She checked her appearance in the mirror. "I meant every word I said in there, OK? And I've already got my eye on someone who can give me everything I want."

"Oh, really?" I said, putting one hand on my hip. "And who might that be?"

She looked at me in the mirror. "You're not going to like it."

I knew she was thinking about Branson, but I didn't want to hear it. I'd seen him and Jewels together around campus, and I'd been wanting to ask her about their relationship. But I didn't feel like this was the time to talk about that. Jewels's cocky attitude had to be dealt with first.

"You know, there's a big difference between self-esteem and arrogance," I said.

"There is?" she joked.

I met her gaze, and she lowered hers.

"Don't worry," she said softly. "I'm not going to put anyone down. That thing with Anna really hurt me and I'm still trying to get over it. But I need to focus on me. If anyone gets mad because I love myself, that's their problem."

She washed her hands, dried them on a paper towel, and threw it in the trash. Then she nudged me back a little and walked out.

After the party, when I returned to my room that night, I read a few more pages of *Secret Keeper*, the book Mom had bought me. It was really helping me to understand who I was in Christ.

Just as I was getting into the chapter, I heard a slight tap on my window. I went over and pulled up the shade, and I couldn't believe my eyes. Branson stood there lip locked with Jewels! She winked at me, like she'd tapped on the window just so I could see her with him.

As much as I cared about her, and as much as I wanted to believe she had changed after the Anna ordeal, I couldn't let this kind of thing go. She was hurting my feelings, and I would have to talk to her about it. Soon.

I pulled down the shade, turned off my light, and cried in the darkness for hours.

The next day, at gymnastics practice, my body wasn't functioning as well as it usually did. I barely felt awake.

"What am I doing wrong?" I asked Nadia.

"Looks like you're trying too hard," she said. "You're letting the pressure of making the team get to you. You've got to relax. Or just stop trying."

"No way," I blurted. "I want to be here. I want to make this team more than anything."

"Then you've got to start enjoying gymnastics again," she advised. "Have fun with it and don't worry so much about what other people think."

Her words encouraged me and so did the assuring smile she gave me. I strutted up to the uneven bars, determined to put Nadia's advice to the test.

As I finished my first flip on the bars, I noticed a black girl standing in the doorway watching us practice. "Who's that?" I asked Nadia, who was spotting me.

She followed the direction I was pointing with my chin. "I don't know," she said. "But she's been hanging out with Summer all morning. I think they might be roommates."

"Is she planning on trying out?" I asked, dropping from the bar.

"I don't think so," Nadia said. "She's probably just here to support her friend." Nadia hopped onto the bar I'd just vacated, and I started spotting her. "Maybe you should get one of your friends to come out and support you," she suggested as she gracefully flipped between the two bars. "Having someone on your side might make you feel a little less uncomfortable in this hostile environment. Could help you relax you a little."

"I don't need anybody to make me feel comfortable," I grumbled.

Summer sauntered up to me, wiping her face with a towel. "It's almost the end of the semester," she reminded me, as if I had forgotten that time was coming close for the coach to make her decision about that last slot. "I'm doing more difficult moves every day, and you're still doing the same old stuff you did in high school. I don't think there's much question about which one of us is gonna make it on the team and who's gonna be asked to leave."

The black girl from the doorway strolled up beside Summer and looked at me with her hands on her hips. "So this is your competition, eh, cous?" She snorted. "You got no problem, girl."

I couldn't believe she had said that to my face. I didn't even know her. "And who are you?" I asked.

"This is my cousin Starr," Summer explained.

The girl extended her hand. She was beautiful, with fair skin and long, wavy ginger-brown hair.

"I hope I didn't hurt your feelings," she purred. "You seem a little flushed."

"Not at all," I said, trying to sound confident. "Your words just give me more motivation to do better. There's no question that the best gymnast will get on the team."

I walked away, hoping no one noticed my knees shaking.

The next day, I woke up with a positive attitude. I was determined to make the team and not to let anything get me down. I'd set the alarm for 5 A.M. so I could get to the gym for an early workout.

When I turned the knob on the bathroom door, I found it locked. I figured Jewels must be in there going through her many primping stages. Usually, she didn't get up until five forty-five.

"Jewels, I need the bathroom," I whispered, trying not to wake up my roommate.

Payton moaned, rolled over, and snuggled deeper under the covers.

I opened the door and there stood Anna. She was much slimmer than before, which under normal circumstances would have been a good thing, but I wondered if the weight loss had happened because of her emotional problems. If so, that wasn't the right way to do it.

She wiped her mouth and flushed the toilet quickly.

"What are you doing?" I asked her.

"Nothing," she mumbled without looking me in the eye.

"When did you get back?"

"Yesterday." She turned on the water and splashed some on her face.

"Can I have a hug?" I asked, wondering why she was acting so distant.

"Not right now," she said, rubbing her face with a towel. "I'm going back to sleep." She walked into her room and closed the door.

The bathroom smelled sour, so I sprayed a little air freshener. It didn't help much.

A couple of days later, I was sitting on the floor of my dorm room doing stretches when the bathroom door opened slowly and Anna crept in. "Do you have a sec?"

"Sure," I said. "Come on in."

She shut the door behind her and sat on the floor beside me. "I want to apologize about the other day. I was feeling really bad. I guess I'm not fully adjusted yet."

"I understand," I assured her. "I'm just glad you're back."

"Thanks."

"Look, I know you're dealing with a lot. And I want you to know you can talk to me about it whenever you're ready to."

She gave me a disgusted look. "Why would I want to talk to you about my problems? You didn't even visit me while I was in the hospital." She picked at the carpet. "Nobody did."

"I wanted to go see you," I said. "I've just been really busy."

I realized how lame my excuse sounded. I was acting just like Jewels. She always had to get her point across in any conversation, even if it meant blocking someone else out. I wasn't so different. I tended to believe that what I had to say should be heard because I thought I knew how to make people's lives better.

"I'm sorry, Anna," I said meekly. "You were right to call me on that. I'm just going to sit here and listen to whatever you want to tell me." I prayed God would give me the right words to say to her when the time was right.

Anna smiled and took a deep breath. "I had a long talk with Payton," she said. "She told me you felt guilty for not talking to me more. I just wanted to tell you that if it hadn't been for you, I probably would have tried to kill myself a lot sooner. Your kind words helped me battle the depression I've felt for years. Your friendship means more to me than you know."

Her eyes started to swell up and get red. "Laurel, the main reason I came over here today was to ask you to keep praying for me."

I got all choked up inside. I wanted to tell her, right then and there, how to accept Jesus Christ into her heart. But God let me know in my spirit that it wasn't the right time yet. So I just nodded to let her know I understood.

"Laurel, I realize you're hurting too."

I looked at her with a quizzical expression, not sure what she was referring to.

"I know you saw Jewels and Branson kissing outside the window. Laurel, Jewels is trying to hurt you. Please don't let her. She doesn't understand your faith, but for some reason she wants to tear it down, just like she broke me down. Don't fall for it. If the God you believe in is real, ask Him for strength."

"Oh, Anna!" I cried out, unable to remain silent. "God is real. And He *has* been giving me strength to get through everything that's been happening in my life. Even when one of my best friends felt so bad about herself she tried to end her own life."

Anna broke down in my arms and we wept together. After several moments, she wiped her damp cheeks with the back of her hand. "I think I'm ready to know that God of yours."

Suddenly Branson and Jewels weren't a bit important to me. God had given me the opportunity to lead this girl to Christ. What an honor! What a blessing!

I grabbed her hand. "There's a verse in the Bible that says that God loved the world so much, He gave His only begotten Son so that whoever believes in Him can have everlasting life."

"I've heard of that," Anna said. "It's John 3:16, isn't it?"

I beamed at her. "That's right."

"But how do I ask Him to come into my life? Do I just say, 'Come in, Jesus'?"

I chuckled. "Sounds too easy, doesn't it? But it really is that simple. Jesus did all the work to pay for our sins by dying on the cross, so all we have to do is accept what He did and ask God to send His Holy Spirit into our hearts."

I held her hand tight, and tears fell from our eyes onto our knuckles. "Can I pray the prayer of salvation with you?" I asked gently.

She nodded. My heart was filled with joy as we bowed our heads.

"Jesus," I started, "my dear friend Anna is ready to know You. Please hear the words of her heart and come into her life and love her as only You can." I squeezed her hand and waited for her to speak.

"I don't know what to say," she whispered.

"Try this. Dear Jesus . . ."

She paused, then repeated after me in a hesitant voice.

"Thank You for dying on the cross to pay the penalty for my sins."

She said the words, stumbling a little over them. But I could tell she was sincere.

"Please come into my heart. Help me to believe in You. Fill me with Your Holy Spirit and bring me peace in my circumstances."

As she repeated each sentence, I felt the Spirit of the Lord fill the room. I knew He was answering my friend's prayer. The God who created the universe and everything in it was coming to dwell in Anna's heart. And I knew she would be changed forever.

After we said amen, we hugged each other tight. I had a new sister in the Lord, and the angels in heaven were having a party!

The next day, as I was returning to the dorm after a particularly grueling day of classes, I saw my dorm monitor, Judy, sitting behind her desk crying. As tired as I was, I had to stop.

"What's the matter?" I asked as I stood at her desk.

She looked up, her face wet with tears. "Someone hit my car," she choked out.

"Were you hurt?" I asked, ready to call 911.

"No," she said, taking a deep breath to calm her sobs. "I wasn't even in the car. When I went to the parking lot to go out for dinner, I discovered the rear end was totally smashed." She looked up at me, her eyes looking more angry than sad. "Whoever did it didn't bother to stick around or come and find me or even leave a note."

"Won't your insurance cover the damage?"

"I only have liability. Laurel, there's no way I can afford to get it fixed. But I can't drive it the way it is. What am I going to do?" Her anger was quickly turning back to despair.

"I'm so sorry," I said, coming around the desk to put my arm around her shoulder.

"It's not your fault," she said with a shrug. "Don't worry about me. I'll be fine."

"Is there anything I can do to help?" I asked.

"No," she said, her slight smile telling me she was glad I offered anyway. "I've got to call the police and report this."

I went up to my room and told Payton about Judy's accident. She acted like she didn't even care. As a matter of fact, she didn't respond to anything I said. I finally decided to leave her alone. I sat at my desk and opened the textbook for a test I had to study for.

A few minutes later, Payton rushed to the bathroom. I could hear her crying through the door. I figured she must have been upset about Dakari and Tad again. I took a deep breath, preparing to hear the whole romantic sob story.

I knocked twice on the bathroom door. Finally Payton let me in. Her hair was mangled and her hands were shaking.

"Laurel," she blurted out, "I'm the one who hit Judy's car."

"What?" I said. "How?"

"Well, it wasn't really me. My friend did it. But she was driving my car!"

"Why did your friend leave instead of calling the police or trying to find the owner?"

"I didn't want her to tell anybody because I was afraid my dad would get mad at me and take away the car." Payton fell to the floor.

I got down in the tight space with her and held her in my arms. "It's all right, Payton. We all make mistakes." I stroked her dark hair. "But you have to tell Judy."

"I know," she said. "I want to pay for the damages. I shouldn't have let my friend drive my car."

"You'd better tell her soon. Judy's about to call the police."

"No!" Payton cried, her eyes wide with fear. "I could go to jail for leaving the scene of an accident!"

"I'll go talk to Judy with you if you want," I offered.

"Thanks," Payton said, breathing a small sigh of relief.

We walked down the hall to see Judy. Payton's steps were slow and hesitant. I knew this was the last thing she wanted to do. But I was proud of her for doing it.

When Payton told Judy the accident was her fault, she was furious. She yelled at her for being irresponsible and fleeing the scene of an accident. But when Payton told Judy she was sorry, she calmed down and they started talking about how to work things out.

Payton didn't tell Judy that someone else had been driving her car. But since she was taking responsibility, I didn't get involved.

When it looked like they could handle things without me, I headed to the gym for practice. As I hurried down the hall, I started talking to God in my mind.

Lord, I thought college was supposed to be fun! There have been some joyous moments, but for the most part everything has been catastrophic. Is this going to get any better?

Everything was weighing me down: gymnastics, Jewels and Branson, my grades. It would be easy to get really depressed. I knew I could just let it all out to God, but I felt incredibly burdened at the moment.

Help me, Lord, I pleaded as I neared the gym door, *because I'm having no fun.*

e L e v e N

listening
for hope

i glanced at my watch as I raced down the hall toward the gym. Realizing that practice had started twenty minutes ago, I picked up my pace even more. I was already on thin ice with Coach Burrows, and I sure didn't need to give her one more reason to choose Summer over me for that last spot on the team.

But some things are more important than practice, I thought. I'd gone with Payton to talk to Judy and helped them work things out. Then I'd had to change for practice. Surely God would bless me for my efforts. After all, I was doing a good deed for somebody.

When I burst into the gym, I noticed no one was warming up. At first I figured everyone was still in the locker room changing. Then I saw them all nestled in a corner, listening to the head coach.

I stood in the doorway for several seconds, wishing I could turn around and walk away. But I forced my feet to tiptoe over to the meeting. As soon as I took the first step on the polished gym floor, Coach Burrows stopped speaking and all eyes turned to me. Some of the girls smirked; others shook their heads.

As I sat on the floor beside Nadia, I was hoping someone would say something reassuring, but no one did.

"That's exactly the kind of thing I'm talking about," the coach said without even looking at me. "Some of you aren't taking this team seriously. We can't win a national championship with mediocrity. I have not seen dynamic routines from any of you. I don't know what's pulling your performance level down, but whatever it is, I'm going to get rid of it."

My hands started sweating. Did she think *I* was the cause of the team's poor performance? Was it I she was planning to get rid of?

"Now, get out there on the mats and warm up."

Everyone stood and silently headed toward their favorite apparatus.

"Shadrach," the coach hollered, "I want to see you."

I walked up to Coach Burrows, my knees shaking and my mouth dry.

"You're very close to being cut," she said, not even whispering. "I want to see something impressive from you, and it had better be soon. Do you understand?"

All I could do was nod. I had been working on some complex routines on the balance beam, but I wasn't ready to show them to her. Still, I knew it was now or never.

"I have been working on some stuff I think you'll like," I told her. "Do you want to see it?"

"I'd love to," she said with an uncharacteristic smile.

As I approached the balance beam with confidence, Coach Burrows stopped to say something to one of the other gymnasts. While I waited for her, I took a lot of deep breaths, staring at the balance beam and praying I'd do well.

"You're not ready," Nadia whispered in my ear. "You

don't have your routine down yet. Let's work on it tonight and you can show her tomorrow."

"Thanks," I said, "but I know I can do this. It's time for me to start believing in myself and in God."

"All right, Shadrach," Coach Burrows said, her arms folded across her chest. "Let's see what you've got."

All the other girls stopped their practice to watch me. I took one last deep breath and prayed one more prayer for God's help. Then I launched into my complex routine. The mount went perfectly, which gave me some measure of confidence. As I hit the first few moves without a hitch, I started to smile. Everything I did was flawless, even one of the moves I hadn't nailed before that very moment.

Thank You, God! Thank You, God! I chanted in my head.

As the moment neared for me to do my back aerial, I knew I would execute it as beautifully as the rest. I soared in the air for a brief moment, relishing the thrill of doing something I loved so much and performing so well.

But at the end of my back aerial, instead of landing on the beam, I fell on the mat, bottom first. My ego was badly bruised, but my tailbone was hurting too. I screamed out in pain.

Some of the girls started snickering. The coach walked away, shaking her head and making notes on her clipboard.

I tried to get up, but the pain was too great. The two trainers who always lingered in the corners of the gym hurried over to help me. I didn't want their assistance, but I couldn't stand on my own.

The trainers carried me to a back room, where they had me lie facedown on a table. One of them poked my bottom to see if anything was broken. "It's just a bad bruise," he said.

The second trainer handed me a bag of ice and told me to leave it on the bruise for a little while. "Take the ice bag home," he suggested, "and ice it down some more."

I had to face reality. I was never going to be a Gym Dawg.

After the trainers left the room, I stared at the floor, trying hard not to cry from the physical and emotional pain. Then I sensed someone beside me. I looked up through teary eyes, hoping Nadia had come to me with some comforting words. Instead I saw Summer Love crouching beside me with a condescending look on her face.

"You might as well quit right now," she whispered with a sneer. Then she walked away, returning to practice as if the end of my world were of no consequence to her at all.

I carefully climbed off the table and stood in the doorway watching everyone else practice. I'd been working hard all semester, yet I couldn't seem to catch up with the other girls. I was good, but they were awesome.

I wanted to go out there and work out some more, but with every step I took, throbbing pain tore through my body.

Summer's words came back to me. *Maybe she's right,* I thought. *Maybe I should quit.*

When gymnastics practice ended and everyone else left, I hobbled back to the dorm. I was relieved to find it empty. I wanted to have a pity party, and that would be easier if I was alone.

I had a hard time getting out of my sweats without making the pain in my backside worse. When I finally managed to get changed into an extralong sorority T-shirt, I dumped fresh ice into the pack the trainer had given me. Then I lay across my bed, facedown, and gingerly placed the ice pack on my bottom. It was cold, but the trainer had insisted it was necessary.

In deep frustration and despair, I picked up my pillow and threw it across the room. It hit the window, which shuddered with a loud bang.

Payton flew in from the bathroom. "What was that?" she cried, her eyes big.

"Sorry," I mumbled.

"I'm glad it's just you," she said as she retrieved my

pillow from the corner. "I thought maybe Dakari had broken the window again."

For some reason, her comment struck me as hysterical and I started laughing. Payton laughed with me, even though she didn't seem to know what was so funny.

She handed my pillow to me. As I took it, my laughter faded. Burying my face in the pillow, I let out a flood of tears. Payton sat beside me and put her arm around me.

"You need to get out," my roommate said.

"I can't go anywhere," I wailed. "I'm in pain!"

"Look, my dad's on his way here. He wants to take me out to dinner tonight, and I thought—"

"No way," I said, interrupting her. "I couldn't possibly sit down in a restaurant."

"Come on," Payton pleaded. "I don't want to go by myself. I'm really on the hot seat with him after that car accident. But if you're there, he won't fuss at me so much."

Before I could respond, the bathroom door opened and Jewels peeked through. "I'm claiming the bathroom at six. Branson's coming over at seven to take me out."

Hearing her throw his name out there like that hurt me even more than seeing them together. Had she forgotten how I felt about him? Did she think he didn't mean anything to me anymore? Was she hurting me intentionally?

Without a word, Payton went to the door and pushed it, gently but hard enough to shove Jewels out of our room. I sat up on my bed, fighting the tears caused by the physical and emotional pain, and leaned my head against the wall. "I can't take this."

"Yes, you can," Payton said, holding my hand.

"I don't want to be here when Branson comes to pick her up for their *date*."

"Then come with me and my dad for dinner," she encouraged me. "Who cares about that jerk anyway? Branson is way too full of himself."

I took the tissue she handed me and blew my nose. "You

know, when I first walked in, and I didn't think you were here, I was glad because I thought I needed to be alone. But now I'm really happy you're here. God knew I needed you. Your strength is amazing."

She laughed. "Girl, I only have strength when I'm talking about somebody else's problems."

I laughed with her. "I know what you mean."

"God gives us what we need to get through the stuff we've got, or He wouldn't give it to us. We just have to stick together and look out for each other, that's all."

Mr. Skky looked just like Payton, only a man and taller. He was really nice. When he found out I'd injured my tailbone at gymnastics practice, he suggested we bring my bed pillow to sit on at the restaurant. I thought it was cool that he didn't worry about being embarrassed by that.

After we ordered our food, Payton's dad asked me how things were going with me. By the time our meals arrived, I had shared just about everything that was happening in my life. As he listened to me ramble on, I realized how much I missed my own father.

"I mean, I don't know how these teachers expect us to master all this stuff so quickly," I complained, cutting into my delicious-smelling piece of teriyaki mahi mahi. "The first year of college shouldn't be so much harder than high school. I never understood before why so many freshmen dropped out and never came back. Now I get it. Just passing the classes seems nearly impossible sometimes."

"Yeah, tell me about it," Payton grumbled, spreading butter on her baked potato.

Her dad looked at her with compassion. "Payton, honey, you've just got to try harder. Being in a majority white school might be uncomfortable, but you have to find a way to adjust and make friends. Maybe you should try out for the cheerleading squad."

"I can't cheer at this school, Dad," Payton said.

"Why not?"

"The flips and jumps are way different. At most black schools, cheerleaders shake and jam. Here they do acrobatics. I can't compete with that."

"I know how you feel," I said to Payton. Then I turned to her father. "It's been really frustrating for me to try to get on the gymnastics team. The other girls seem like they've been doing the harder tricks for a much longer time than I have."

"Both of you young ladies need to stop talking about what you can't do. You're going through a big transition, just like all the other freshmen. How you handle it is what counts."

I took a bite of my steamed broccoli. It was delicious. Just as the tasty food was providing nutrition to my body, I knew Payton's father's words were providing nutrition for my spirit.

"You both love the Lord," he said. "You need to lean on Him. With your schoolwork, your extracurricular activities . . . even with the boys."

"Oh, Dad," Payton said, rolling her eyes.

But I knew he was right. I'd told him a little about my situation with Jewels and Branson, and he already had a pretty good idea of what was going on between Tad and Dakari in Payton's life. I really wanted to hear what advice Mr. Skky had for us. And I could tell Payton did too.

"What do you think we should do about these guys who are messing up our lives?" I said, spearing another bite of fish.

"Nothing," he said.

"Nothing?" Payton echoed.

"That's right," he said with a smile. "Just leave them alone. Guys want to be with girls who have it together. I'm not saying you need to get yourself straightened out just so you can get a guy. But when you're a basket case emotionally, you drive the good ones away."

"Why can't they help us get our lives figured out?" I asked. It made sense to me.

He smiled. "Because they're still working on themselves. A boy can't help you if he doesn't have his own act together."

Payton and I glanced at each other and laughed. We both knew the guys we'd been stressing over needed to work on themselves a lot.

"When somebody you think cares about you starts going out with someone else," he said, "especially if it's someone close to you, you might think he's doing it just to make you mad. And maybe that's what Branson is doing. I don't know. But it might be that he's simply trying to figure out his own life, just like you're trying to figure out yours."

"But somebody who really cares about you wouldn't play with your heart like that," Payton interjected. "Even if he was going out with someone else, he'd try to keep it subtle to spare your feelings, right?"

"Absolutely," Mr. Skky said. "You girls deserve to have good guys, and that's what you need to be on the lookout for. A real man is going to only want to be with you."

"Sounds good to me," Payton exclaimed with a smirk.

"You know any guys like that?" I asked her, grinning.

"Nope," she said. "You?"

"Nope." We both turned to Payton's dad.

He chuckled. "Maybe the guys around you just aren't mature enough yet. They're only freshmen, after all."

"So, what do we do while we're waiting for these guys to grow up?" Payton asked, her eyebrows raised.

"Just enjoy your life. Have fun finding out who you are. The rest will come at the right time."

"I sure hope so," Payton said.

"Make your heavenly Father proud," Mr. Skky advised us. "If you do that, your earthly parents will be proud as well."

Payton got up out of her chair and hugged her dad. I sure missed mine. But I was thankful that God let me borrow Payton's father for the evening, to feed hope into my hungry soul.

A couple of days after my pep talk with Payton's dad, I started singing in the bathroom. My bottom felt better and the swelling had gone down. I'd just turned in a paper that I felt I did a pretty good job on. I was starting to care less about Branson and wanting to be closer to God. I was so thankful that I broke out in a song of joy.

Then I realized that the song in my head was playing on the radio in my room. I flew out of the bathroom to turn up the volume. The song was called "Imagine," and it made me think about what heaven will be like and what I'll be like when I get there. It made me long for the day when I would fall to my knees and praise God forever and ever.

The lyrics also reminded me that there was more in my future than this life on earth. I needed to focus on heaven, not the concerns of this world . . . to live for God, not just myself.

"Hey, could you turn that down?" Jewels grumbled, standing in the bathroom doorway.

"Sure," I said, accommodating her request with a smile. "No problem."

She stood in the doorway, staring at me. "Branson and I are going to study at his fraternity house, and I—"

"That's nice," I said politely, starting to sort the freshly washed clothes in my laundry basket.

"I might stay overnight at the sorority house," she added coyly.

"Cool," I said in a sweet tone, tossing my socks and underwear into the drawer.

She looked confused, undoubtedly wondering about the change in my demeanor, probably thinking I was putting on a false front. But with God's protection, it honestly didn't hurt me as much to hear about Branson and Jewels. Sure, if I could have it my way, they wouldn't be seeing each other. But her life was not mine to live, and neither was his.

I wasn't going to let myself get bruised by their actions. Those days were over.

I set up the ironing board and plugged in the iron, then turned to Jewels. "You don't have to tell me about what you and Branson do. You guys obviously have a connection. But I don't need to know about it."

"Whatever," she said, still looking perplexed.

"I do wonder why you keep telling me about him. I thought you and I were friends, but I guess that's not the case. A true friend wouldn't flaunt a relationship with my ex-boyfriend in front of me the way you do."

I arranged my green cotton blouse on the ironing board and started pressing it, turning my back to Jewels. I heard her huff a few times, then stomp out of the room and slam the bathroom door.

With my worries about Jewels and Branson finally off my mind, I determined to pick up my grades. As soon as my laundry chores were completed, I said to myself, *Library, here I come!*

As I entered the big, quiet room, I headed straight toward my usual seat. My mystery guy hadn't been there the last couple of times. But I kept going back to that table where we'd met. I didn't really want him to be there. He was a distraction, and I needed to be focused. But when I saw him sitting in his usual chair, looking even cuter than I remembered, I didn't mind the diversion a bit.

When he saw me he got up quickly. "Am I in your seat?" he asked, gathering his books.

"No," I said, "this is your table." I started to walk off.

"There's room for both of us," he said.

As I put my bag on the table, I noticed the jogging suit he was wearing sported the school's colors.

We studied in silence for a few minutes. Then someone tapped me on the shoulder. I looked up and saw it was the guy with the goatee and sideburns who'd argued with me about the Bulldawgs football game. His friends from the time before were all sitting at the desk next to my table.

"So, how's Miss Kicker Fan today?" he asked. His face looked even hairier than I remembered.

"Leave her alone, Denny," his buddy said.

I laughed. "It's OK. I do like Hanson. I'm proud of that guy."

Denny sat down with his friends, who started snickering at him. "So," I said to the group at the desk, "do you think we're going to make it to the play-offs this year?"

"I hope so," the cute guy at my table answered, getting into the conversation.

"We need somebody who can make big plays," Denny put in.

"A lot depends on the kicker, I think," I said.

"Hanson is pretty good," Denny commented. "For a freshman."

"Yeah, he is," I said.

"Did you see the interview of him in the school newspaper?" Denny asked.

"No," I said. But before I could ask for details, his friend stood. "Come on, Den Man, we've got to get back to the frat house."

Denny stood, and so did his friends. As the others gathered their books, he started writing something on a piece of notebook paper. While everyone else in his group headed for the exit, Denny came up to me and handed me the paper. "Here's my number," he said. "Maybe we could go to a game together. I'm sure we'd have a lot of fun."

Denny winked at me, then followed his friends out of the library. As I dropped his number into my book bag, I noticed the cute guy at my table watching me.

"He's crazy," I said, feeling embarrassed for some reason.

Determined to get back to studying, I rummaged through my book bag for a textbook. The one I wanted was underneath my Bible, so I placed it on the table.

"I knew there was something special about you," the cute guy said.

"What do you mean?" I asked, pulling out the textbook I planned to study.

He picked up my Bible and held it up. "I'm a Christian too."

I smiled and he grinned back.

"I'm still growing in my faith, though," he said, putting my Bible back on the table.

"Me too," I said, forgetting all about my textbook. "You know, I don't even know your name."

He laughed. "I don't know yours either." He leaned his arms on the table. "What do I look like to you?"

"Oh, I love playing the name-guessing game." I placed my hand on my chin and stared at his face. "Let's see. I'd say you're a . . . Charlie. Chuck? No, Charlie. Definitely."

He raised his eyebrows. "Are you saying I have a big blob head like Charlie Brown?"

"Of course not!" I said, laughing with him.

"Well, if I'm Charlie Brown, then you've got to be Lucy."

"Fair enough," I said. "Hey, did Lucy and Charlie ever date?"

"Yeah, I think they started in elementary school."

We giggled like a couple of kindergarteners.

"You know," Charlie said, "I think Hanson is a Christian too."

"What makes you say that?"

"Oh, just a comment he made in the interview for the school paper."

"I've got to get a copy of that," I said, half expecting him to offer me his. But he didn't.

"I'm sure he felt your prayers for him during that last game," Charlie added. "The article said he was really nervous about the kick."

"That guy?" I said. "He looked completely sure of himself out there. I wish I had his confidence."

"Don't talk down about yourself like that," Charlie said. "Everything I've seen you do exudes confidence. The way you defend other people, the way you show you care. You're a beautiful girl on the outside, but you're golden on the inside because you're related to the King. He lives in you, and you've got His strength."

I soaked in his words, my hand cupped firmly on my chin. He was a believer and he was saying what I needed to hear. I really wanted to apply the truth he was telling me to my life.

I knew God had led both of us to this library at the same time because I needed to hear what he had to say. We really connected and not just because our conversation focused on grades or dating or football. It was about listening for hope.

twelve

enjoying
the break

i couldn't believe I was sitting in the campus library listening to a college guy talk about the Lord with zeal, love, and respect. It gave me goose bumps.

"I hope I'm not boring you," the guy I'd nicknamed Charlie said.

"No way," I said quickly.

"I know you came to the library to study," he said in an apologetic tone, "and here I am going on and on about my Christian beliefs. I'm sorry."

"Don't be," I said. "I like listening to you talk about God. Please go on."

Charlie rubbed his hands over the soft leather cover of my Bible. "I can really relate to what David wrote in Psalm 10. At the beginning he was angry with God. He wanted something but wasn't getting it."

"I know what you mean," I said, remembering how many times that psalm had ministered to my heart.

"In the middle of the psalm, David praises God even though he still doesn't have what he wants. Then, in the last couple of verses, God blessed him for trusting Him." He looked up at me, his eyes intense. "There are things I want that I don't have. So I wonder what I'm doing to block my blessings."

I'd never thought of life that way. Could I be doing something to block my blessings too?

"I'm starting to feel a little like Job," Charlie went on. "I've got my life pretty much on track. Because of my full college schedule, I can't go to church as often as I'd like, but I go to Sunday services every week. I don't have a job, so I can't tithe money, but I get up early and give the Lord the first hour of my morning. I feel confident that my heart is pure. And yet most of the time I feel like I'm still learning what it means to trust the Lord. I guess I'm in kind of a growth period. Have you ever felt like that?"

I realized he wasn't asking me about doctrinal issues but about my own Christian walk. As I contemplated how to answer his question, I pondered a few things about myself. Did I feel like all the stuff I'd been going through over the last semester happened because I brought it all on myself? Or did I feel like a model Christian just going through trials because God wanted to teach me to trust Him through them?

"I can relate," I assured him. "I mean, I'm not perfect, of course. But most of the time I feel compassionate toward people around me who are suffering. You know, like Hanson, the kicker. I don't even know him, but I really empathize with him because I understand the pressure he's under. My roommates are going through a whole bunch of difficult stuff, and I try to listen and respond to them in love."

He leaned closer, listening intently.

"I had a boyfriend last year," I told him. "But we broke up because I wanted to stay pure for God, and he didn't understand that."

His eyes flashed. "Hey, any guy who can't understand you wanting to please God above pleasing him shouldn't be in your life."

I could have reached over and hugged the guy, and not just because he was so cute. He understood my battle with temptation and agreed with my decision.

"I've fought the desires of the flesh too, but I finally conquered them through prayer and a strong focus on God. Now I feel like I'm in control of my temptations to sin but still going through painful trials."

"I feel that way too," I said, amazed that we were in such similar places in our spiritual walks. I can practically hear God telling Satan, 'Whatever you do to her, she's still gonna love Me.' But then Satan breathes on me and I go crying to God, 'Why me?' I can feel His Spirit inside, and I know He's right there with me. Trials don't necessarily come because of anything I'm doing wrong. Sometimes it's just my cross to bear. When I think about Jesus carrying His cross all the way to Calvary for me, my burdens don't seem so hard, especially when I give them all to Him. Does that make sense?"

"Perfect sense," he said. "I can be thankful that God is with me and that He's faithful in carrying me through my trials."

An alarm started beeping, and Charlie checked his watch.

"Aw, man, I've got to go. I have a 10:00 curfew."

"Oh, gosh, so do I," I said, shocked that the time had flown so fast.

We started packing up our books, and before I knew it, Charlie was gone. I stood there for a moment, then closed my eyes and bowed my head to pray for him. Just before I said *Amen* in my mind, I felt the presence of someone near me, interrupting my silent prayer.

When I opened my eyes, I was pleased and surprised to see Charlie standing there grinning at me.

"Were you praying for me?" he asked.

I shrugged and smiled.

"Wow," he said. "God really is in my life. I'm glad He sent me here to meet you."

I tried not to blush. "Why did you come back?"

"I realized I hadn't wished you a Happy Thanksgiving. So I came back to give you that blessing, and I got a blessing instead. That's pretty cool."

It felt so good that he considered me a blessing, I didn't know what to say.

"I have to confess," he said, "I came back for another reason too."

"What's that?"

"To see if I could walk you back to your dorm."

"Oh, no, thanks," I said. "I think I can find my own room."

"It's getting pretty late," he argued. "I wouldn't want anything to happen to you."

"I'll be OK," I said, chafing a little at the implication that I wasn't capable of taking care of myself or at least trusting God to take care of me.

He hesitated, and I realized that he hadn't meant to imply anything negative about me. He seemed to genuinely want to walk me to my dorm just to spend more time with me and out of concern for my welfare. Besides, it probably was unwise for me to wander around campus alone so close to curfew.

"All right," I said, gathering my stuff.

We walked out of the library together. Chatting all the way, I began to feel like I'd known Charlie my whole life. In the moonlit night I felt a strong urge to place my hand in his, even though our relationship wasn't at that level.

When we got close to my dorm, he stopped and said, "Thanks. I feel really blessed that God allowed me to meet you."

"I feel blessed by you too," I said.

"Good night."

For a moment I wished he would kiss me. But he turned slowly and walked away. I watched him for a while, then went into the dorm building.

It felt great to be able to give someone advice that was good for me as well. My first semester hadn't gone the way I'd planned, and maybe that meant I needed to get myself more seriously connected to God. Then again, maybe I was doing fine. Either way, I was going to have trials until the day I joined Him in heaven. As long as I called on the Lord every second of the day, every step of the way, I could bear any burden. My Savior loved me more than life itself. And for that, I was truly thankful.

I went home for Thanksgiving weekend, and seconds after my arrival, my old friends Meagan and Brittany came over. I was so excited! They had missed me as much as I missed them, and they couldn't wait to whisk me off somewhere to hang out and have fun.

My mom seemed disappointed that I was taking off as soon as I arrived. She probably would have been happy if I did nothing for the whole break except stay by her side.

"A bunch of us are getting together at the bowling alley, Mrs. Shadrach," Brittany said sweetly. "I promise I'll have Laurel back soon."

Mom hesitated but finally said, "All right. I know you girls need your time together too." Then she turned to me. "Try not to stay out too late."

I rolled my eyes but promised to get back at a reasonable hour.

"I love your tans," I told my friends as soon as we were bundled into Brittany's Mustang. "That Florida sun must suit you."

"We've been lying on the beach every day after class," Meagan confessed with a giggle.

I had a fleeting moment of jealousy, but deep in my heart I was glad my friends were happy.

We drove first to the Dairy Queen for chili dogs, french fries, and ice cream sundaes.

"So, who's gonna be at this bowling party?" I asked, scraping the last of the hot fudge out of the plastic cup.

Brittany rattled off a list of names of people I remembered from high school. When I heard Branson's name, I sat up straight in my seat.

"I don't want to be anywhere he is," I said. "Not even close."

"Oh, don't be such a spoilsport," Brittany said. "You can ignore him if you want."

"Don't you get it?" I practically shouted. "I don't want to go if he's going to be there."

"Come on, Laurel," Meagan begged. "It'll be fun."

I took a deep breath. "If you guys want to go, that's fine. I'll just walk home from here." I grabbed my purse and headed out the door.

Brittany and Meagan followed me into the parking lot. "All right," Brittany said, grabbing my elbow. "What's been going on between you and Branson?"

I looked at Meagan, hoping she would help me out by changing the subject. But she looked just as curious as Brittany.

I really didn't want to go into my lack of a love relationship with Branson. But I didn't see that I had much choice.

"I kind of had a rerun of what happened with you last year, Britt."

"One of your new friends is going out with him?" Meagan asked, almost smiling.

"I wouldn't call her a friend exactly, but she is one of my suite mates, and yes, she and Branson are dating."

"Oh, then we are definitely going to the bowling alley," Brittany said, pulling me toward her car. "That boy needs to be told off."

154

She stuffed me into the backseat and drove to the bowling alley parking lot. I spotted Branson's blue Camaro right away. "I'm not going in there."

My friends begged and pleaded for me to change my mind, but I held my ground. "You know, this is how we got into all that trouble last summer at the fraternity house. I insisted on going home, but you two talked me into going with those guys who tried to attack us."

"Hey," Brittany said, "you can't blame that on us."

"Laurel's right, though," Meagan said, steering away from a rehash of one of our most frightening experiences together. "If she doesn't want to go in, we shouldn't force her."

"You two can stay in the car if you want," Brittany said, hopping out of the driver's seat. "But I have something to say to that jerk Branson. After all the heartache he put Laurel through in high school, he's not going to do it again. Not to my friend. No, sir."

She slammed the door shut, leaving Meagan and me in her car. I was glad the fall weather was mild because she didn't leave the keys. We couldn't have turned on the heat or the air conditioning if we'd needed to.

"Now, why did she have to do that?" I hollered, my stomach churning. "It's over between me and Branson. He's humiliated me for the last time. I don't need her to fight my battles."

"Just calm down," Meagan advised me.

"I can't," I said, feeling queasier by the minute. "Every time I think Branson Price is out of my system, he gets me all worked up again."

"Take a few deep breaths," she suggested.

I knew Meagan was right. I didn't want Branson back, but questions of self-doubt flooded my mind. Why did he keep turning to other girls, especially ones who were close to me? Wasn't I good enough for him? Did he do it just to spite and hurt me?

I felt the Dairy Queen chili dog threatening to come up, so

I opened the door and squatted on the pavement. Sure enough, within seconds, my dinner was all over the parking lot.

"Are you OK?" Meagan asked, handing me a Dairy Queen napkin from the car.

"Does it look like I'm OK?" I said, wiping my face with the napkin.

Just as I was about to get back in the car, I felt my stomach churning again. I turned back around, and more of my meal came up.

"Meagan," I said, my head pounding, "can you go in there and get Brittany? Tell her I need to go home."

Meagan looked at me with a curious expression. "Oh, my gosh, Laurel, are you pregnant? Is that why you're so bummed out about Branson? Is he saying it's not his kid?"

"No," I grumbled, climbing into the backseat. "It's nothing like that."

"I thought you were going to be a virgin until you were married. I guess college really does make people grow up fast."

I didn't have the strength to continue arguing with her. I just lay on the black leather interior and moaned.

"I wasn't gonna tell you this," Meagan whispered, "but I lost my virginity too. Thank goodness he used protection. But I didn't really enjoy it. Did you?"

"Meagan," I groaned, "I'm not pregnant, OK? I'm still a virgin."

"Oh, I see," my friend said as if she didn't believe me.

"Look, can you just go get Brittany? Please?"

"All right," she said. Meagan got out of the car and closed the door gently. I lay back in the seat, holding my stomach. *Stupid chili dog,* I thought. *Who'd have thought anyone could get food poisoning from the Dairy Queen?* Then again, maybe I was just getting the flu or something.

But the more I thought about it, the more sure I felt that my problem wasn't food poisoning or flu. My stomach was just reacting to all the pressures in my life.

While I waited for Meagan to get back with Brittany, I

prayed, my whispers sounding loud in the enclosed car.

"Lord, You've got to help me. I can't even have a good time with my friends without feeling knots in my stomach from anxiety, stress, and worry. I try to focus on You, but all these little roadblocks keep getting in my way."

A knock on the window startled me. I looked up and saw Brittany standing beside the car, with Meagan behind her. Brittany opened the door and whispered, "Branson's coming this way."

For some stupid reason, I felt an overwhelming desire to fix myself up. I pushed my hair back so it wouldn't look so mangled, straightened out my wrinkled clothes, then grabbed a mint out of my purse and popped it into my mouth.

I had no idea what he wanted to say to me, or why I cared so much. His actions had said everything already. When I saw him walking toward me, I took a deep breath.

"I don't want to talk to him," I said to Brittany from the backseat.

"You need to," Brittany said. "He's got some things to say that you need to hear."

When Branson got to the hood of the car, Meagan placed her hands against his chest, stopping him. He continued pushing, but she held him back with a determined look on her face.

"She's got it all wrong," I heard Branson say. "Please let me talk to her."

"I'm sorry," Meagan said, her voice full of understanding and compassion. "But she doesn't want to talk to you right now. Maybe tomorrow. You guys definitely need to straighten things out between you before you go back to school." She lowered her voice to a whisper. "You're gonna at least have to decide what to do about the baby."

I couldn't believe she'd said that.

"Laurel's pregnant?" Branson cried out, his eyes wide.

"Oh, my gosh!" Brittany squealed, bending down and leaning into the car. "You're pregnant!"

"No, I'm not—" I started, but the look in her eyes told me she didn't believe me any more than Meagan had. She stood and glared at Branson.

"Brittany," I moaned, still feeling too sick to my stomach to get out of the car, "I don't want to see him."

She walked over to him anyway and yanked him to the side of the car. With my head pounding and my stomach churning and my forehead sweating, I lay back against the seat and closed my eyes.

Branson climbed into the front and looked at me from between the bucket seats. "I can't believe this. We broke up because you wouldn't sleep with me, and then you just give yourself to the first boy you meet at college? Who's the guy?"

"Why should I tell you anything?" I said, peeved at his demanding attitude.

"Because I deserve some answers. That should be my baby you're carrying."

Brittany and Meagan were staring at us like they were watching a soap opera. The looks on their faces made me want to laugh.

I knew my friends cared about what happened to me, and Branson obviously did too. I didn't want him back, but it felt good to know he still cared.

"Look, you guys," I said, "I'm not pregnant, OK? I just got sick on a chili dog."

Branson blinked a few times, then looked outside at Brittany. They both gazed at Meagan. She shrugged and tried to look innocent. Then everyone's attention came back to me.

"You should all see yourselves," I said, starting to giggle at their confused expressions. Brittany's lips curled into a smile, then she began chuckling. Pretty soon we were all laughing like hysterical idiots.

Yeah, this Thanksgiving wasn't going to be bad at all. It didn't matter what else happened because I was enjoying the break.

studying
pays off

"So you're not really pregnant?" Branson asked when the laughter died down.

"No," I practically screamed. "How loud do I have to say it?"

I turned away from everyone's stares. The three of them had me trapped inside the car, and my stomach was still rumbling.

Branson shifted in the front seat, still trying to converse with me in the backseat. "Brittany told me you think I'm dating Jewels."

"I've seen you pick her up from the dorm."

Branson shook his head. "I don't know what she's told you, but we go to a study group together. I've been picking her up because she said her car was in the shop."

I stared him down. "I saw you kiss her outside my dorm room."

His cheeks reddened. "She told me she lost a dare and she had to kiss me."

I was dumbfounded. Apparently Branson didn't have any romantic feelings for Jewels after all. She had fabricated the whole thing.

I should never have taken Jewels's word at face value. In the future I would have to do my own research to find out if what she said was true. Jewels sure needed to know the Lord.

"I'm sorry," I said to Branson.

"Laurel, even though we aren't together anymore, I don't want us to hate each other."

"Me either," I said as I reached between the bucket seats to take his hand. I looked up at my girlfriends. "Can you take me home now, Brittany? I don't want to get sick in this parking lot again."

Brittany thumbed for Branson to get out of the car, and he did. Then she and Meagan hopped in. I smiled at Branson as Brittany peeled out. He waved back.

I didn't know what was going to happen with Branson and me. But for the first time I was content with not knowing.

I counted the people: twenty-eight. Four fewer than there were place settings. As I was about to ask my mom who else was coming, the doorbell rang.

"Laurel, honey," my mother called from the kitchen, "can you get the door?"

"Sure," I said, wondering who the late arrivals might be.

When I opened the door, my jaw dropped. There stood Foster McDowell, my boyfriend from senior year, with his parents and his sister, Faigyn.

"Hello, Laurel," Mrs. McDowell greeted me with a big hug. Mr. McDowell followed her into the house.

"Hi," Faigyn said, also giving me a hug before she came inside.

Foster hugged me tightly too. He was still very handsome, and I'd missed him a lot. But I was glad his embrace brought nothing more than feelings of friendship.

I invited Foster to sit in the living room with me. Although we were surrounded by friends and family, we talked a lot about our past fun times together.

All too soon, my mom called, "Dinner's ready." The food smelled awesome, but I was really having a good time talking with Foster.

I took my usual seat beside my dad. Foster sat next to me. We had a ball laughing and continuing to talk about old times. When the people around us broke into their own conversations, Foster asked, "Have you been in the Word this semester?"

I had just taken a bite of potato-corn casserole, so I didn't respond right away.

"How is your spiritual life?" he asked before I could answer his first question.

"It's growing," I said after swallowing the delicious morsel.

"Are you dating someone seriously?"

I looked around at all the relatives enjoying Thanksgiving dinner. "I'd really rather not go into that right now," I said quietly.

"OK," he said graciously. "I can understand that." After a pause, he announced, "I'm dating someone."

"I'm happy for you," I said. And surprisingly, I meant it. I didn't feel jealous at all. Foster deserved someone who could really be into him. And I was glad he was still my friend.

"Let's raise our glasses," my dad said, lifting his glass of iced tea, "and toast to whatever we're thankful for."

Dad starting off by proclaiming his gratitude that his family was all under one roof again. The toasts continued around the table, everyone naming one thing. I was grateful for so much that when my turn came, I summed up everything by saying, "I'm thankful that I found myself worthy in Christ."

Everyone fell silent. I felt as if I'd said something wrong.

But then my father said, "I'm thankful for that too," and he took a big sip of his tea.

Everyone cracked up.

After dinner a group of us played charades. My team beat my brothers' team by five points. A rematch was called for, but Foster pulled me aside and asked if I was ready to have a serious talk.

We went back to the living room. At first neither of us knew what to say. To break the ice, I gave him the quick version of my first semester.

"Wow," he said. "You've been through a lot. But it seems like you found your anchor."

"Yeah, I have," I said.

"Don't worry about the gymnastics thing. It's going to work out the way it's supposed to. And so is your relationship with Branson. Just release him and let God guide you to whoever you're supposed to be with."

I was glad we could talk about what was going on in our lives, as friends, and encourage each other with godly counsel as brother and sister in Christ.

Just then Mrs. McDowell came in. "Sorry to interrupt your conversation, Foster, but we have to go."

"All right, Mom," he said. She left us alone to say our good-byes. When we hugged each other, I thanked God for our friendship.

I spent most of the next day in my room studying for exams. As I sat in my comfortable old chair trying to focus on my psychology textbook, I found myself wishing I were in the library studying with Charlie.

"How's my girl?" my dad said, startling me with his sudden presence.

I looked up and saw him standing in my doorway, just like old times. "Daddy," I said, getting up and hugging my father to let him know how much I had missed him. He sat on my bed, and I returned to the chair facing him.

"How have you been, sweetie?"

"I'm fine, Dad," I said.

"Laurel, I want you to know I'm very proud of you," Dad told me. "From what you've told me, you've been through a lot at school this year." He grinned. "And you probably haven't told me everything."

I smiled back at him. "God's taking care of me," I assured him, taking his big hand in my smaller ones. "Your prayers for me are getting through."

My dad winked at me. "You're right," he said with confidence. "God's got you." He squeezed my hand. "I love you, Laurel."

"I love you too, Dad."

He stood. "Well, I'll let you get back to your studying." He shuffled to the door, turned, and gave me a big smile, then shut the door. I knew I'd made my father's day.

I'd had such a great Thanksgiving, part of me didn't want to leave my home. But another part of me was ready to go back to college. This time, I felt I was a little tougher and more prepared than before. And I only had a couple of weeks before I could come home again for Christmas break. I didn't figure much could possibly happen in that short a time.

———————

"Laurel, can you please zip me up?" Jewels called from the bathroom.

I didn't feel like helping her with anything since she'd been lying to me about Branson. I didn't want to be cruel, and I knew I should address the issue with her. But I had no desire to do that. So I just determined not to let her get to me.

"I'm on my way out," I called back to her. "I really don't have time to help you right now."

"Wait," she begged, coming into the room with her dress unzipped. "I've got a hot date again with you-know-who." She winked at me. "It'll only take a second to zip me." She turned around, sticking her naked back in my face.

"No, I don't know who," I said, zipping her up so quickly I almost caught the metal teeth in the silk. "Who is it?"

"I don't want to rub it in, Laurel," she said, sounding for all the world like she was being a sweet, compassionate friend.

"I'd really like to know," I told her.

"Well, if you insist," she said, adjusting her dress in my mirror. "I'm going out with Branson again. I think he really likes me." She turned to me. "Does that bother you?"

"If you mean, 'Am I jealous?' no. I'm learning to trust God with whatever happens in my life. If Branson wants to be with someone else, that's fine with me. No big deal."

"I'm so glad," she said, laying her hand on my arm as if she still thought I needed consoling.

I decided to ask a few pointed questions to see if I could get her to admit to her deception. "So, are you driving or is he?" I asked.

"A lady never drives on a date," she said.

"I'm sure if he knew how nice your brand-new Mustang is, he'd want to drive it instead of that clunky blue Camaro of his."

Her face turned almost as red as her dress. "My car isn't all that nice. We don't need to show it to him."

"Why not? I'm sure he'll love it."

"I just—" she sputtered. "I don't want to drive. It's tacky for the girl to drive on a date."

She was obviously lying, but she wasn't about to admit it, so I decided to end the game. "The truth is, you told Branson your car is in the shop."

"Why would you say that?" she said, sweat forming above her crimson lips.

"You guys aren't dating. You're studying. He's picking you up but for a study group, not a date."

Jewels's face turned red, but she didn't say a word.

"Why have you been lying to me?" When she didn't answer, I said, "I thought we were friends."

"We are," she whined.

"No," I said, shaking my head. "You're too selfish to care

about anyone besides yourself, and that's not my idea of a friend."

I grabbed my books and slammed the door behind me.

"You're later than usual," Charlie said as I approached our favorite spot in the library. "I was afraid you weren't coming."

I smiled. I knew he'd be waiting for me. We'd been meeting in the library every night for a couple of months. We got a lot of studying done, but we were getting to know each other too.

I dropped into the chair with a huff, unable to get my mind off my problems with Jewels.

"You seem really agitated," he said. "Didn't your Thanksgiving break go well?"

"That's not it," I said. "I actually got answers about a lot of things while I was there."

"Do you want to tell me about it? I don't mean to pry. But I'm here to listen if you want to talk."

I did need someone to open up to, and I decided Charlie was the perfect choice. He wouldn't have any hidden agendas, and I knew he wouldn't judge me.

"My suite mate is a barracuda," I blurted out.

He laughed so loud that the people at the next table gave us a dirty look. "What do you mean?" he asked more quietly.

"She's been telling me that my ex-boyfriend has been coming on to her and making me think they're all hot and heavy. But I found out over Thanksgiving break that they're not together at all."

"So, are you upset that she was going out with your ex or that she's not really dating him?"

"I'm mad that she lied to me. I really cared about her."

"And you don't care anymore because she lied?"

"That's bad, I know. I mean, as a Christian, shouldn't I still love her?"

"Is she a believer?"

"No," I answered, wondering why that mattered.

"Then you've got to show her how a Christian would respond in this situation. You know, when friends let me down, I try not to lash out at them in the flesh but to respond to them in the Spirit. That way they can see something in me that's different from what's in them, and hopefully they'll want that."

"Wow," I said. "You're not just a studier of the Word. You're a doer."

He smiled. "That's why I study. So I can be transformed by His power. If you don't get deep into God's Word, it's easy to blow like the wind when trouble comes. Psalm 1:3 says, 'Be like a tree planted firm, unmovable.' That means you focus on God's will instead of your own, even when someone lets you down."

I was thrilled that he cared enough to encourage me.

"It's like your exams. You've been studying all semester, so you'll probably ace those tests. Whatever you put in comes out. It's the same way in the Christian walk. Psalm 118, the longest book in the Bible, has 176 verses—"

"Yeah, I know," I said. Growing up as a preacher's kid, I had learned a lot of facts about the Bible.

"That psalm talks about the Lord opening our eyes so we can understand what's in His Word. Then the Holy Spirit can work in our lives. We need to not only read Scripture but study it until we understand it. Only then can it protect us from spiritual harm. If you really know the Bible, whenever you're in a situation where you need God's help, the Holy Spirit can bring to your remembrance the appropriate passages that you've hidden in your heart."

"I know what you mean," I said. "When times are tough for me, sometimes a Bible verse will suddenly pop into my head, and it's always one I memorized somewhere along the way, even though I usually complained about having to memorize it in the first place."

He smiled. "See?" he said. "All that studying pays off."

f o u r t e e n

decorating
with care

I stared at Charlie across the library table. This guy really intrigued me. He was fit, though not as buff as some of the guys I'd known. And he was helping me grow in God's Word, which was awesome. He wasn't judgmental. He didn't lecture me for having feelings that weren't of the Lord, like Foster used to. He even took a deep interest in making sure that I was OK. I could hardly believe this guy was real.

We were supposed to be studying, but he took the time to make sure I had a smile on my face. He even pulled out two cold bottles of water from his bag and handed one to me. When he asked me about my day, he really listened. Unlike Branson.

I can't like this guy, I told myself as he moved his chair closer. *None of this can be real. Love never happens this easily. Besides, am I really over Branson?*

My greatest concern with Charlie was that I didn't know if he was interested in me in a romantic way. Sure, he was being nice and listening attentively. But maybe he was just doing his Christian duty.

"I'll be right back," I said and headed to the bathroom.

I went into a stall and prayed. *Lord, I place Charlie in Your hands. I don't want to have any expectations. But I feel something for him that . . . well, I can't explain. Make me feel what You want me to feel, not what I want to feel.*

I washed my hands and checked out my appearance in the mirror. I wanted to look adorable for Charlie, so I put on a little lipstick before going back to the table. When I got there, I saw that Charlie had vanished and all of his books were gone. I peeked down a couple of aisles, but he was nowhere in sight. I finally just plopped down into the chair and opened my textbook.

After a few minutes someone tapped me on the shoulder. I smiled when I turned around and saw Charlie. He was grinning from ear to ear.

"You looking for me?" he asked.

"Maybe," I responded coyly.

"You seemed kind of sad that I was gone."

"Don't flatter yourself," I teased.

He untucked his T-shirt and brought the hem of it up to my face. Instinctively I moved away. With his other hand he gently held my head steady, then slowly brought the shirt up to my lips.

"What are you doing?" I asked, caught off guard by his actions and by the peek I got of his muscular abs.

"You had lipstick on your cheek," he said, showing me the pink mark on his shirt. "I just wanted to get it off."

As he sat down next to me, I thought of the prayer I'd just prayed. *Lord, I told You I didn't want any feelings that aren't supposed to be there, and here he is touching my lips!* I could barely breathe.

He put his arm around the back of my chair. He smelled wonderful.

"You're not trying to impress me, are you?" I asked,

gently removing his arm from around my shoulders.

"Of course not." He folded his hands in front of him on the table. "Just trying to be a gentleman. You wouldn't want to walk out of this library with lipstick on your cheek, would you?"

"No," I said quietly.

"So, did my gesture score points with you?"

"Are you kidding?" I teased.

We continued going back and forth in the lighthearted banter of close friends. This was a unique relationship, and God was answering my prayers, allowing me to stay focused on Him.

If gorgeous, warmhearted Charlie was my gift from the Lord, I didn't want to just tear open the wrapping paper and throw it in the trash without appreciating every single crease in the beautiful paper that surrounded him. It wasn't time to open the present yet. I didn't even know if the present was mine. But I could enjoy the box it was in. I could enjoy the moment God had given us and be thankful for my newfound brother in Christ.

When we went our separate ways, I realized how much I would miss Charlie over the Christmas break. I had become stronger through our time together. The Lord had allowed him to be in my life to help me realize that my self-worth was in Christ. If I studied God's Word, things would always turn out all right. So I was determined to do that and to pray for my dear friend.

When I opened the door to my dorm room, I saw somebody fumbling through my dresser drawer. I flipped on the lights and recognized my intruder.

"Jewels!" I yelled.

She looked up at me with a startled expression. "You scared me."

"What are you doing in my drawer?"

"I chickened out," she said in a gloomy tone. She pulled a little green heart-shaped box out of my drawer and handed it to me. "I wanted to let you know how sorry I am, but I didn't know how to give this to you. So I was just going to leave it here and let you find it."

"You got me a gift?"

"There's a note taped to the bottom. I was hoping, after you read it, maybe we could talk."

"I don't know, Jewels," I said, staring at the box. "A lot has happened. A gift can't buy my friendship."

"I'm sorry. You're right. I always do the wrong thing. But I have good intentions, really."

I closed my drawer, unsure what to say to her.

"I'll leave you alone now," she said. "Just forget I was here. If you don't want the gift, you can throw it in the trash." She headed toward the bathroom.

"Wait," I said.

Jewels turned around. The caring look in her eye seemed sincere.

Charlie and I had just been talking about living the Word and being a good example to others. I wanted so much for Jewels to know the Lord. And yet here I was, being hard on her, not giving her a chance to explain, not offering her grace. I had to accept her, regardless of whether or not her heart was pure. I had to let the Lord work on her. Even though she had done a lot to make me hate her, I couldn't act like the world and cast her out of my life. I needed to work on this friendship.

I hugged her. "Thanks," I said, looking at the box. "That was sweet."

"You haven't even opened it yet. Maybe you won't like it."

"It doesn't matter what's inside. It means a lot to me that you thought to get me something. I appreciate that, Jewels. And believe it or not, I appreciate you."

"It doesn't seem like it sometimes."

"You're right," I said. "I have been tough on you, but that's because I care. You have a lot going for you, and I'm not talking about your family status, your sorority, money, or your beautiful looks. All those things are neat to have, but I'm concerned about what's inside you."

"I know this gift won't make amends between us," she said. "But I really want to apologize for telling you that I had a big thing with Branson when we were really just study partners."

I sat on my bed and invited her to join me. "I'm sorry too," I said as she perched on the edge of my mattress.

"For what?"

"You said I've gone after some things you thought were yours. So let's call it even, all right? When we come back from Christmas, we can start fresh."

"I'd like that." Jewels smiled. "So, do you want to open the gift now?"

"Sure," I said. I opened the heart-shaped box and found a silver ring with a cross on it. "Wow," I said, putting it on my right index finger. "This is gorgeous." I looked up at her. "Thank you so much."

"No problem." Jewels shrugged. "I'm glad you like it." She stood. "So, are we OK now?"

"Yeah," I said. "We are."

She gave me a big smile, then went back toward her room. As she passed through the bathroom, I heard her say under her breath, "Gosh, that prayer thing actually works."

Jewels's been praying? That's awesome!

I sat on my bed and stared at the ring on my finger. *Thank You, Lord, for helping me not to blow that one. Thanks for continuing to use me in spite of myself. I count it all joy to be used for Your glory. I love You, Lord. Oh, how I love You.*

"I can't believe Jewels let us take her car," I said to Mandelyn and Jill. Exams were finally over, so we'd decided to celebrate by going into town for some shopping. Almost all of the professors had posted grades already, and I'd received mostly Bs. Of course, As would have been better, and I was hoping to improve my next-semester grades with a lot more studying. But I was satisfied with my Bs because it sure could have been worse.

"I think she agreed to let us use the car for shopping because she hopes we'll get something for her," Jill joked, steering carefully around a corner.

"That's not nice," Mandelyn replied. "Jewels has really changed lately."

"You're right," Jill said. "I don't know what got into her, but she really has been nice to everyone the last few days."

"That's a refreshing change," I said in a grumpy voice.

"Hey," Jill said, going a little too fast and almost running a stoplight. "It's Christmas time. You should be happy. Excited."

"You'd better start paying attention," I said, buckling my seat belt. "You don't want to get a ticket or wreck this car. Keep your eyes on the road."

"What's your problem?" Mandelyn asked from the front passenger seat.

"I don't know," I said. "Guess I'm just not in the mood for shopping."

"Not in the mood for shopping?" Jill echoed as if she couldn't imagine that even being a possibility.

"Are you going home for the holiday?" Mandelyn asked.

"Yeah," I said. "My mom's coming by this evening to pick me up."

"And that doesn't have you psyched?"

"I am excited about it. I guess it just doesn't seem like Christmas to me yet. Maybe when I get home and have some of my mom's hot cider, it'll feel more right."

Our first stop was the Christian bookstore. The place was beautiful. It was covered with decorations, wreaths, lights, trees, ornaments, fake snow, and crosses. In the middle of the store, a group of people dressed in authentic-looking costumes portrayed the nativity scene. They looked so real, I almost bowed down to worship the "baby Jesus."

Suddenly I realized why it hadn't felt like Christmas. I hadn't put up any decorations in my new home. I loved giving God praise through decorating for His Son's birthday. I couldn't leave school without doing something special to my room.

As I was looking at the wreaths, Mandelyn and Jill came up to me with mischievous smiles. "Oh, my goodness," Jill said. "The cutest guy in the world just walked into the store."

"You guys are supposed to be shopping for Christmas gifts, not guys," I said.

They looked at me like they thought I was being way too self-righteous.

"I'm just kidding. Show me this fine man."

They led me down the greeting card aisle, stopping near the end and pointing toward the rack of CDs.

My mouth fell open when I saw Charlie standing there. He picked up a CD, stared at the back for a moment, then looked up and peered in our direction. The girls quickly pulled me away.

"We don't want him to see us looking." Jill giggled.

"I'm going to go talk to him," Mandelyn said, peeking around the calendar display.

"No way," Jill said, pulling her back. "I'm going to talk to him."

The two of them argued back and forth about who was going to make the first move. When they finally got up enough courage to do something, their dreamboat had disappeared.

I went back to the aisle with the Christmas decorations. As I was checking the price tag on a beautiful snow globe, I felt a tap on my shoulder. When I turned around, Charlie was standing there, smiling at me.

"Hey," I said.

"What a coincidence to find you here," he said.

We made small talk for a while, then said good-bye. I felt a small pain in my heart at the realization that I wouldn't see him again until after Christmas break.

"I'll be thinking about you," he said as he left.

My heart danced.

Seconds after Charlie walked away, my friends came up to me. "Oh, so you know the guy, huh?" Jill said.

"Way to hold out on us asked Laurel," Mandelyn added.

"He's a friend," I explained, walking toward the fiction shelves.

"Looked to me like you both want to be more than just friends," Jill said, picking up a book.

"What do you mean?" I asked, taking the novel out of her hand.

"You like him and he likes you." Mandelyn turned to Jill. "Why can't we find a good one like that?"

Jill took back the novel and walked up to the cash register with it. Mandelyn joined her and bought a CD. I purchased the wreath I'd been admiring.

Jill drove us to the mall, where we shopped for a couple of hours. I found all the gifts I needed and got great deals on everything.

On the ride home, with several shopping bags on the seat next to me, I felt filled with the Christmas spirit. I was thankful that I'd had a chance to see Charlie once more before the break.

As soon as I got back to the dorm, I started to hang the wreath on our hallway door. As I was banging in the nail, Payton came up the hall.

She stopped in front of me. "We're going home today. Why are you decorating?"

"It's just my way of giving honor to God," I said. "Maybe this wreath will serve as a reminder to someone that we're celebrating the birth of the Savior." I tapped the bell on the wreath and heard it tinkle. "Don't you think that bell just shouts, 'Hallelujah! Praise the Lord! A King is born'?"

Payton smiled and shook her head. But I knew she understood what I was saying.

"It's a little crooked, huh?" I said, standing back and looking at my work.

As Payton helped me straighten the wreath, I realized that Christmas for me was holy and special. It was all about Jesus and I was not going to take it lightly. Hanging ornaments was a way to show the Lord how much His love meant to me.

I looked again at my beautiful wreath. It was perfect.

After we went inside our room, I said to Payton, "You're gonna come to my house sometime over the break and spend the night, right?"

"I don't know," she said hesitantly.

"Oh, come on," I urged. "You're going to be in Conyers anyway visiting your grandparents. You can at least come over for one day."

"I'll let you know, OK?" Payton said as she pulled out her suitcase from the closet.

I was bummed that she was acting so apprehensive, but I didn't want to be pushy. If God worked it out for her to want to come, great. If not, I was willing to be patient.

Our moms arrived around five o'clock to pick us up. When I hugged Payton good-bye, she asked, "Is the invite still open to come for a visit?"

"Of course it is," I said, ecstatic that she'd changed her mind.

"I'll call you when I get to my grandma's," she said.

"Sounds great."

On the way home my mom filled me in on how my family had been. She said that she and Dad were happy I was coming home because all three of my brothers were having trouble.

Liam, the oldest, who was a senior in high school, had

spent all of his savings to record a demo album he could send to Christian recording companies to try to get a music deal. He did it without asking my parents about it and without researching the market. It turned out the so-called producer was running a scam. The guy collected $4200 up front, then didn't show up at the studio to record the music. Not only was Liam out all that money, but he still didn't have a demo.

Luke, my youngest brother, who was a high school sophomore, got his first D because he didn't study for a test he thought he didn't have to prepare for. But Luke was dating Faigyn, Foster's sister, so things like studying, school, and grades weren't as important to him as they used to be.

"He's growing up," I teased my mom.

She chuckled. "Well, he won't get a chance to grow up if he keeps getting grades like that. I'm going to kill him."

We enjoyed a good laugh together. Then she said, "Lance got suspended."

"What did he do?" I asked, wondering what trouble my sixteen-year-old middle brother had gotten into this time.

"He was caught making out with a college-aged substitute teacher. Honestly, Laurel, I don't know if your brother's a virgin anymore."

I cleared my throat. "You know, Mom, most high school boys today aren't pure."

"I realize that," she said softly. "But I had hoped my sons would be the exception."

It hurt to see my mom so sad, but I was glad I'd kept my virginity. "Maybe you should just talk to him," I suggested.

"He never listens to anything your dad or I say to him. I was hoping you could speak to him. Maybe you can talk to all three of your brothers."

"I'll try," I said. It made me feel good to think that Mom thought I would have something positive to say to my brothers. I cared about them deeply, and I knew that whatever I said to them would come from love and compassion.

I hoped I could help get them back on the right track.

"Quite frankly," Mom continued, "we thought you were a handful. But now that you've left, it seems like our problems are just beginning."

I chuckled.

As we neared home, my heart leapt at the sight of all the beautiful Christmas lights on the outside of our house.

"We decided to wait until you got home to put up the tree," Mom said.

When we pulled into the driveway, I saw my brother Luke standing in the doorway, waving at me. I scrambled out of the car and rushed up to him. I gave all of my brothers big hugs as I entered the warmth of the living room.

My dad held his arms open wide to welcome me into a hug too. But his embrace ended too quickly. Something was wrong.

"Let's get the tree decorated," I suggested. "I'll go pop some corn so we can make a long strand. You guys can put up the tree." My family stared at me with long faces. "What's wrong with you people?" I asked. "We're supposed to be celebrating the birth of our Savior."

Mom came in from the car with my two small suitcases. "Go ahead and tell her," she said quietly.

Dad took my arm. "Honey, my father's in the hospital."

I collapsed into the nearest chair. "What happened?"

"We're not sure," Mom said. "The doctors think he may have had a stroke, but they aren't saying much else. Your grandma's really worried."

"I'm sorry, honey," Dad said, "but we have to change our holiday plans. I know you were looking forward to staying here for Christmas this year, but we need to head up to Arkansas day after tomorrow."

"Of course," I said. "No problem."

My dad walked out of the room, mumbling something about needing to pray. I knew he was worried. My grandfather had never asked Jesus into his heart, so he didn't have the assurance of salvation that my brothers and my parents and I had.

We didn't need to be in Arkansas to get my grandfather saved. If we couldn't witness to him, God would find another way. But Granddad was not going to leave this earth without knowing the Lord. I just knew it.

"We've got to decorate the house tonight," I said. My mother and brothers stared at me like I was crazy. "That might sound weird, but we've got to keep each other lifted up. And if we're leaving soon, we have to do it now."

"You're right," Mom said. "Let's do it."

Mom went to the kitchen and started making our traditional holiday treat: gingerbread cookies and hot apple cider. Lance ran upstairs to get the artificial tree out of the attic. Liam put some Christmas music on the stereo. Luke helped me untangle the lights that had been put away improperly last Christmas.

In a few short moments, we were all gathered in the living room, listening to yuletide music, sipping cider, and putting up decorations. The strand of popcorn wound its way around decorations from years past.

Things had been kind of haywire during my first semester in college, and being with my family felt good. I remembered many happy Christmases in my childhood. I knew this one would have more wonderful memories because the season of Christmas wasn't about gifts under the tree. It wasn't about having the best decorations on the block. It was about bonding and treating your family with love—the love of the Savior, the kind of love the heavenly Father showed us by sending His Son to die for our sins.

After the tree was decorated, we called Dad from the basement. When he came into the living room, we plugged in the tree lights, held hands, and sang "Jesus Loves Me" in unison. It was like the Holy Spirit was getting charged within us, needing just a little power boost to shine brightly in our hearts.

The phone rang, bringing our wonderful moment to an abrupt end. No one wanted to move, but we knew someone needed to answer the phone. A lump rose in my throat.

"I'll get it," I said, hoping it would be good news.

Boy, was I surprised when I heard Branson Price say hello.

"I hope I didn't interrupt anything," he said.

"We're kind of having family time," I said. Everyone was staring at me, waiting to find out if the call was about Grandpa. "It's for me," I said, waving them off. When they kept watching me, I turned around so I could have a bit of privacy. "What's going on?" I asked.

"I know Christmas is your favorite time of the year. So I wanted to see if maybe I could take you to breakfast tomorrow."

Without even thinking I said, "Sure. Be here at eight."

"I'll see you then," he said.

I hung up the phone, then turned back to the tree. "There's something missing," I said. Then I realized what it was. "There's no star at the top."

My dad smiled, then brought out the star from behind his back. I smiled at him.

Dad let me climb on his shoulders, and Lance and Liam spotted me to make sure I didn't fall. Luke unplugged the lights so I wouldn't get shocked. I placed the star on top of the tree. When Mom flicked the lights back on, we all oohed and aahed about how beautiful our house looked, not just because of the great decorations but because we had decorated everything with such tenderness. Even my strong brothers, who couldn't usually care less about this stuff, took it seriously this time.

I had missed my family. We all loved the Lord, and we had something special, even in the tough times. Giving all we had for God made the night bright. I was thankful that we spent our night decorating with care.

fifteen

possessing true happiness

"breakfast is ready," my mom said as she peeked into my room. "You want to help me set the table?"

"I'm sorry, Mom," I said, brushing my hair. "I forgot to tell you; Branson wants to take me to breakfast. He says he needs to talk."

I half expected my mom to say I couldn't go. But I was in college now, making my own decisions, and I didn't really have to ask permission from my parents anymore. Still, I was back home and I wanted to show respect for them. So I asked, "Is that OK with you?"

"Absolutely," my mom said. "You look beautiful."

"It's just breakfast," I said, blushing at her compliment. "Branson and I are just friends, and I'm fine with that."

My brother Luke came into the room and handed me the phone.

"Hello?" I said after he and my mom left.

"I'm out in your driveway," Branson said. "Should I come to the door? Or am I on your family's bad list?"

I chuckled at his thoughtfulness. "I'll be right out."

"Your family hates me, don't they?" he asked.

"No," I assured him. "I haven't told them all the details of what we've been through."

"Thanks," he said.

"I'll be out in a sec," I told him, then hung up the phone.

Any other time I would have wanted Branson to be a gentleman and call for me at the door and say hi to my parents and my brothers. But things like that didn't matter to me like they had before. We weren't dating, so there was no need for the formality.

I ran a brush through my hair, then scurried down the stairs. As I opened the front door, my dad asked, "Where are you off to?"

"Branson and I are going out to get a bite to eat," I said. "I won't be gone long."

"I hope not," my dad said. "We're heading off for Arkansas first thing tomorrow morning."

"I know." I kissed his cheek. "I love you, Dad."

"I love you too."

Branson got out of his car and opened the passenger door for me. "You look great."

"Thanks," I said, blushing as I fastened my seat belt.

"Thank you for going to breakfast with me. Anywhere in particular you'd like to go?"

"O'Charley's?" I suggested.

As Branson drove to the restaurant, I wondered what he had in mind. Was he trying to smooth talk me for some reason? I hoped not, because I wasn't ready for anything with him but a good breakfast.

When Branson parked the car, I quickly opened my door. I didn't want him to think this was a date.

The restaurant was crowded but cozy. Branson ordered French toast and I asked for eggs Benedict. While we waited for our food to be delivered, I talked about my sorority, the football team, what classes I expected to take next semester.

"You're not letting me get a word in edgewise," he said. "You've been dominating the conversation, but you haven't said anything about us."

I hesitated, not sure what to say. Should I be direct? I didn't want to hurt his feelings. I hushed up and let him speak.

"My first semester at Georgia," Branson said, "I thought about you a lot. I kept thinking that if I had you in my life, my grades wouldn't be so bad. And maybe I would have tried out for the football team."

"I thought you were planning to do a walk-on," I said, remembering the day we went to the college together over the summer and spoke to our separate coaches.

"I didn't have the courage without you in my corner telling me I could do it. It was like my cheerleading squad was gone. I've really missed you, Laurel. I mean, you live right around the corner from me, and every time I drive past your dorm I want to stop and see you. At first I thought I was just lonely. But then I realized that what I was feeling for you was real. I know we have our issues to deal with, especially about how far to take our relationship sexually. But I have finally realized that I want to be with you, even if all we can do is hold hands and talk.

"Laurel, I'm not going to lie to you. I have . . . been intimate with other girls since we broke up."

I gulped, taking in the impact of his statement. "Thanks for being honest," I finally said.

"But it was really disappointing because it wasn't with you. A couple of times I imagined I was with you even while I was kissing someone else."

A few months ago hearing that he'd had sex with other girls would have destroyed my heart. But the confident, self-assured feelings that flooded my soul confirmed that I was completely over him. I was sure of who I was in Christ.

Because the Lord was everything to me, I didn't have to settle for anything less than His perfect gifts for me. And Branson wasn't that.

I did want to show him God's love, however, and not act like a snot. "I've missed you too, Branson. At the beginning of the semester, I felt really depressed about us not being together."

His eyes lit up.

"However, I have come to realize that I don't need to be dependent on you. I have to depend on the Lord. I can't afford to take any more gambles in my life, and you and I getting back together would be a major gamble."

He stared at his plate. "Why did you agree to have breakfast with me?"

"I don't want us to be strangers. Besides, I thought this could be the beginning of us figuring out what kind of relationship we can have."

I expected him to say, *"Forget this; you can walk home,"* like he did in high school when he left me in the parking lot after I refused to have sex with him in the car.

"Friends, huh?" he said. "OK. I'd rather have that than nothing."

I got up from my chair, went over to his side of the table, and gave him a friendly hug.

I was so excited. I had taken a stand for Christ and gained a friend.

"What do you mean, you're tired of school?" I said to Brittany over the phone later that afternoon.

"College is hard work," she said, "and it seems pointless. I mean, HIV could end my life tomorrow. It just doesn't seem like it's worth the effort."

I'd always admired Brittany's strength and courage. But the disease she contracted in her senior year of high school had chipped away at her strong personality. Since we didn't go to the same college, I hadn't realized how low her confidence level had sunk.

"You're right," I said, sprawling across my bed. "You did mess up pretty bad."

"Thanks a lot," she said.

"But that doesn't have to be the end of the story. You still have a future. You're taking your medication, right?"

"Yeah."

"And who's to say that scientists won't find a cure any day now?"

"That sure would be great," she said, her voice filled with hope.

"Besides, none of us know how long we have to live. I could be hit by a car or something."

"How can you say that?" she said.

"Because God has promised me a better life than the one I'm living now. I don't have to worry. I can just live for today. I'm excited about what He's given me, not concerned about what I don't have."

I paused to say a quick prayer for guidance, then continued. "You know, I used to envy the fact that you always had new clothes and lots of money and you could do whatever you wanted. But then I realized that my worth wasn't in material possessions. My worth is in Christ."

"I wish I had your confidence," she said.

I shot up another quick prayer. "Britt, remember when you accepted Christ last year? You said you wanted to change some of your ways. You were so full of passion for God that you wanted to follow Him with your whole heart."

"I remember," she said. "But I didn't stick to my vow."

I sat up on my bed and took a deep breath. "You didn't change at all after you gave your life to Christ. Becoming a Christian doesn't take all your problems away, but if it's real, it makes you different."

"So I'm not a saint," she said defensively.

"I'm not saying you need to be perfect," I explained.

"But you've got to put some effort into your relationship with Christ in order to get something out of it." I paused, waiting for her to speak.

"I'm listening," she said. "Go on."

"God wants to do so much for you. He wants to live and reign and to be sovereign in your life. He wants the Holy Spirit to shine bright through you."

"How can I make that happen?" Brittany asked.

"You've got to let Him show you that you're worth something. Pray, go to church on a regular basis, get in a Bible study group, things like that." I started pacing around my room. "A lot of freshmen flunk out of school. But you got Bs. That's great! You need to go back next semester focused—not on other people but on God, yourself, and your dreams."

"My doctor told me that people with HIV need to try to stay upbeat so the cells won't take over."

"All the more reason to remain positive," I said, sitting back down on my bed.

"You're right," she answered.

"Now, go and grow with God, girl. Read the Word. Let Jesus Christ reign in your life. Ask Him to show you what He wants you to do. If you look at your life through the Lord's eyes, you won't have to worry about tomorrow."

"When you get back from your grandma's, we've got to hook up," she said.

"I'd like that."

After we hung up, I went outside and found that my family was barbecuing. As I started to set the backyard table with plastic plates and cups, an unexpected visitor showed up. It was Robyn, my black friend from high school. I raced up to her, gave her a huge hug, and told her how glad I was to see her.

My mom invited her to join us, and she happily accepted a plate with hot dogs and potato chips. Then she whispered to me, "Can we take our food over to the hammock? I need to talk."

"Sure," I said.

"I hate my school," she blurted out when we were alone. "I don't want to be there anymore."

I couldn't believe I was hearing the same words Brittany had just said.

"I want to go to Georgia."

"Why?"

"Well, for one thing, I miss my old boyfriend, Jackson. Do you ever see him?"

"Of course," I said. "He's on the football team."

"He's probably got plenty of girls around him all the time."

"You can't choose a college just because you want to follow some boy," I said, then popped a chip into my mouth.

"That's not the only reason."

I swallowed the salty snack. "What else?"

"I really like my all-black school, but I've done nothing except party there."

"Oh, so your grades have been taking a nosedive, huh?" I took a bite of my hot dog.

"Actually I have a 3.69."

I almost choked on my food. "You mean your GPA is higher than mine and you haven't studied?"

"It doesn't take much effort for me to do well there. But that's the problem. I need to be challenged more. Basically I'm just repeating the stuff we did in high school."

"I like that reason better," I said.

"I thought going to Fort Valley would help me discover who I am. But now I realize that I already know who I am. I'm excited about being black. I don't need to be in an isolated environment to feel that way. I want to be in a college that's more like the real world."

"If that's your reason, I support it," I said, setting my plate on the ground. "So, are you going to apply for a transfer?"

"Already did. And I got accepted into Georgia. I'm gonna be with you next semester."

"Really? That's great!" We gave each other a high five.

"I don't know if I'll be happier there than at Fort Valley, but I want to at least try UGA."

I hugged her. "I can't wait to introduce you to my roommate, Payton Skky. She's a black girl and she reminds me so much of you. I'm sure the two of you will hit it off really well."

We both went back for more hot dogs. Then we played a game of kickball with my brothers. Before Robyn left, she promised to pray for my grandpa. We agreed to get together when I got back from Arkansas.

Later that evening Meagan came over to pick me up for Christmas Eve service. I could tell from the red in her eyes that she'd been crying. When we got in the car, I asked her what was wrong.

"I'm dropping out of school," she said.

My heart was heavy. I knew a lot of freshmen dropped out in the first year, but I couldn't believe that three people I knew all wanted to leave. "Why?"

"I don't want to talk about it right now," she said.

I didn't press. I decided to wait until she was ready.

When we got to the church parking lot, Meagan broke into tears. "I'm pregnant."

I didn't know what to say. I reached out and held her hand.

"At Thanksgiving, when I thought you were pregnant, I was actually excited about it because I didn't want to be alone."

"Who's the father?" I asked.

She lowered her head. "I'm not sure."

"What?" I shrieked.

"I only did it a couple of times," she said quickly. "But each time was with a different guy. So I'm not sure which one got me pregnant."

"Meagan," I groaned.

"I wish I'd listened to God's Word and waited. Brittany's

experience should have taught me about consequences. But it didn't." She buried her face in her hands.

"What are you going to do now?" I asked, wondering if I would have to talk her out of considering abortion.

"I'm dropping out of school to have this baby."

"You don't have to do that," I said.

"Come on, Laurel," Meagan said. "I don't want go back to college and hang out with my friends while I'm pregnant."

I could see her point. Meagan and I cried together some more. Then I prayed with her. "Lord, please give my friend strength and courage. Forgive her for her sins, as You've forgiven me for mine. Somehow make this wrong turn out right. Make something good come out of this. In Jesus' name. Amen."

"So I guess you're going to have to get a job so you can raise your child, huh?"

"Actually, Laurel, I've decided to give the baby up for adoption."

"Really?" I said. "How does that work?"

"I found a Christian agency that helps young mothers go through the process," Meagan explained. "They'll help me with everything I need, even a place to stay and emotional support. The social worker there has been a real blessing."

"It sounds like God is working things out for you," I said.

Meagan nodded. "I just wish I wouldn't have messed up, you know?"

"Don't worry about the past. Most girls who mess up don't make up for what they did wrong by doing something so right."

"Do you really think I'm doing the right thing?" she asked, tears spilling down her cheeks.

"Absolutely. You're not ending the life of that little person inside you just because you're afraid he's going to ruin your life, like some girls do. You're going to make sure he has a good home with parents who will love him and take care of him better than you can at this stage in your life."

"Do you think my child will hate me someday?"

"No way," I assured her. "He'd probably hate you if you never gave him a chance to live. But you're not going to do that. When you see him in glory, he'll be really excited that you gave him the opportunity to live. I'm proud of you, Meagan."

She took a deep breath. "I'm not proud of myself for what I did. But it does feel good to do something unselfish for someone else."

"Have you told Britt yet?"

"I don't know how to. She can be so judgmental."

"Don't worry about it. She's got her own stuff to deal with."

"Thanks, Laurel," Meagan said, her eyes wet with tears.

"Just remember," I said, "God is a God of grace. Your sin is as far as the east is from the west."

All through the Christmas Eve service, Meagan stood close to me. I kept smiling at her and assuring her that everything was going to be OK.

"You are a child of the King," my dad preached to the congregation.

It felt good to be back in the familiar sanctuary of my family's church. As we worshiped the Lord through praise music, I raised my hands high, thanking the Lord for His many blessings, full of joy that He didn't hold our sins against us. He'd sent His Son to die for me so my sins could be washed away with the blood Jesus shed for me on Calvary. Celebrating Christmas, Jesus' birthday, was a wonderful thing.

"In this life," my dad said, pulling my focus back to the message, "there will be turmoil. That's just the way of this world. So how can we have joy? How can we be happy when we're surrounded by sadness and sickness and death? When you've lost your job, or you've been betrayed, when you go through a divorce, where there's no food on the table? How can we feel joy when we can't meet the financial needs of our families, or when we let our friends down? When we sin, how can we feel good about ourselves? It's easy, in such times, to feel like we're unworthy to be in God's family."

I looked at Meagan, sitting beside me. She seemed totally absorbed in the message.

"God loved us so much that He sent His only Son to earth to conquer the grave. Our joy comes not from our circumstances but because of who God is and what He has done for us. We can be happy in spite of the despair all around us because the Lord is with us through the turmoil. We can praise Him even when there's not a song in our heart because we know our heavenly Father is in control of every phase of our lives. Happiness isn't found in our circumstances. True joy is in God."

My dad was putting into words exactly what I'd been feeling for the last few weeks. I had been seeking God daily, and because He was first in my life, I was happy. He was allowing me to minister to people. He was making an impact in this world through me. He provided me with my daily bread. I was thankful that He had adopted me into His family. I was a child of the King!

My first semester of college had been crazy. Leaving my family, losing my boyfriend, doing horrible in gymnastics, studying extra hard just to get a decent grade, dealing with a roommate from another race and a suite mate who was in a different economic class, having a person I knew try to commit suicide, and another person in my dorm murdered because of poor life choices. Going through all that, I had gotten my perspective back to where it needed to be. God went with me to college, but I had fallen away from Him.

When I started walking with Him again, I let Him carry me through the valley.

I couldn't be sad about it all. I could only see God's light. I knew Christ had died for my sins. I could feel the Holy Spirit inside me. I could do anything. I was not going to waver anymore. I was going to be the Christian God wanted me to be. I didn't know what would happen next semester or the next day for that matter. But I knew, at that moment, I was possessing true happiness.

Laurel Shadrach Series

Purity Reigns

Laurel Shadrach is looking forward to her senior year being picture perfect! Her optimism turns sour when Branson begins to pressure her. She wants to keep the man she loves, but making a choice between obeying God and giving in to the desires of her flesh is difficult. Will Laurel let her desires for Branson come between her and God? Will the pressure she feels from Branson destroy her relationships with her family and friends? Will Laurel have the courage to say no to the man she loves?

ISBN: 0-8024-4035-5

Totally Free

There is never a dull moment in the ever-changing events of Laurel's life as she finds herself dealing with the effects of alcohol abuse on friends, family, and a community; a brother who is controlled by the excitement of gambling; and the peer pressures of giving in to sexual urges. Will Laurel continue to bear this heavy burden of secrecy and tolerance alone? Will the Lord show Himself faithful even in these difficult situations?

ISBN: 0-8024-4036-3

Equally Yoked

Laurel Shadrach's world may be a lot of things, but it's never boring. The last few weeks of her senior year are packed with gymnastics meets, parties, final exams, and family. But life topples Laurel's neatly stacked pyramid of plans. Laurel has always clung to faith in a loving God. But a jumble of disappointments and tragedies has shaken her to her foundations. Will her faith stand up to the pressure? Will God prove Himself good and kind even in the worst times life can offer?

ISBN: 0-8024-4037-1

Finally Sure

Laurel Shadrach begins her second semester as a University of Georgia fresh-man with two clouds hanging over her head. First, her grandfather is dying...and second she is in serious danger of being cut from the gymnastics team, which means she'll lose the critical scholarship money that would keep her at the presti-gious university.

The semester is destined to be one of vic-tories and defeats for Laurel. She'll see death up close—not once but twice.

ISBN: 0-8024-4039-8

MOODY
PUBLISHERS
THE NAME YOU CAN TRUST.

1-800-678-6928 www.MoodyPublishers.org

ABSOLUTELY WORTHY TEAM

ACQUIRING EDITOR:
Greg Thornton

COPY EDITOR:
Kathy Ide

BACK COVER COPY:
Julie-Allyson Ieron, Joy Media

COVER DESIGN:
Ragont Design

INTERIOR DESIGN:
Ragont Design

PRINTING AND BINDING:
Bethany Press International

The typeface for the text of this book is
Berkeley